TALES OF MYSTERY & T

General Editor: David Stuart Davies

ORIENTAL GHOST STORIES

ORIENTAL GHOST STORIES

from

KWAIDAN, IN GHOSTLY JAPAN,
and SOME CHINESE GHOSTS

Translated by

Lafcadio Hearn

with an introduction by
David Stuart Davies

WORDSWORTH EDITIONS

For my husband
ANTHONY JOHN RANSON
with love from your wife, the publisher.
Eternally grateful for your unconditional love,
not just for me but for our children,
Simon, Andrew and Nichola Trayler

Readers who are interested in other titles from
Wordsworth Editions are invited to visit our website at
www.wordsworth-editions.com

For our latest list and a full mail-order service contact
Bibliophile Books, 5 Thomas Road, London E14 7BN
Tel: +44 0207 515 9222 Fax: +44 0207 538 4115
e-mail: orders@bibliophilebooks.com

This edition published 2007 by
Wordsworth Editions Limited
8B East Street, Ware, Hertfordshire SG12 9HJ

ISBN 978 1 84022 610 2

Wordsworth® is a registered trademark of
Wordsworth Editions Limited,
the company founded by Michael Trayler in 1987

Typeset in Great Britain by Chrissie Madden
Printed by Clays Ltd, St Ives plc

CONTENTS

INTRODUCTION

From the point of view of his life and his approach to writing, Lafcadio Hearn is perhaps the most unusual of all ghost-story writers. I appreciate that this is rather a grand claim, but allow me to set before you the facts that prompt me to reach such a conclusion.

Lafcadio Hearn was born on 27 June 1850 on the Greek Ionian Island of Leucadia (pronounced Lefcadia – hence the author's first adopted name). His father was an Irishman, Charles Hearn, a Surgeon-Major of King's County Ireland, and his mother was Greek. Young Hearn had a rather casual education but was for a time at Ushaw Roman Catholic College in Durham. However, the religious teachings of his youth had little long-lasting effect on his spiritual thinking. For a great deal of his life he was an atheist. Indeed his rejection of Catholicism helped him to develop into an imaginative and independent young man.

At the age of nineteen, being thrown on his own devices, he sailed to America where he took up newspaper work. The details concerning this period of his life are vague, but for a time he settled in New Orleans (1877–1887), writing for one of the newspapers there, *The Daily Item*. His idiosyncratic column demonstrated his growing romantic and morbid fantasies. He is on record as saying that the 'twin idea running through [my articles] is – Love and Death'. Ideal topics, one might suppose, for an embryonic ghost-story writer.

Hearn also worked for the *Times Democrat* in New Orleans and they sent him for two years as a correspondent to the West Indies. On his return, he was briefly married to an American but she secured a divorce from him rather quickly.

Already we can see that from the beginning Hearn was exposed to many different cultural influences: an Irish father, a Greek mother, an English Catholic education, living in the Creole city of New Orleans, spending time in the West Indies, and experiencing the American domestic scene. It would seem that the main effect that this rich mix of experiences had on Hearn was to foster within him a desire to escape the hedonistic materialism of the West, a desire which eventually led the writer to travel to Japan in 1890. Here his search for beauty, tranquillity, for pleasing customs and lasting values, ended and he remained there for the rest of his life.

Lafcadio Hearn married a Japanese girl and became a Japanese citizen, taking the name Yakumo Koizumi. He also embraced Buddhism as his true faith. In the country of the rising sun, this sensitive writer had found the ideal environment for his temperament and imagination. He secured work as a teacher of English at Tokyo University and became the great interpreter of all things Japanese for the West. His keen intellect and poetic imagination permitted him to understand and interpret sympathetically all things Japanese. This wayward Bohemian genius who had seen life in so many climes and had turned from Roman Catholic to atheist and then to Buddhist, was curiously qualified among those who were 'interpreting' the new and old Japan to the Western world.

I hope now you can understand why I began this essay with the claim that Lafcadio Hearn was the most unusual of ghost-story writers. His greatest achievements in this field were his oriental ghost tales which often re-interpreted versions of Japanese and Chinese legends and folktales. They are utterly devoid of the Gothic trappings so typical of most writing in the genre in the late Victorian period. Their tone, elegance and subject-matter make them unique. It is not so surprising that although he wrote in English, Hearn is still revered as a Japanese writer.

Lafcadio Hearn's approach to the ghost story is so unlike the work of other writers of the Victorian period such as Le Fanu, Bram Stoker, and E. Nesbit, M.R. James *et al*. His narratives have none of the manufactured tension, calculated horrors and lengthy descriptions that feature in the work of those authors. Hearn's style is simplistic and spare, as are his plots, with the stories often taking on the tone and format of a parable. But it is in their simplicity and sometimes naiveté that their power lies. Often there are neither shocks nor frightening moments in his tales because the appearance of the spirit is not regarded as unusual or even unexpected. For Hearn, who referred to his narratives as 'stories and studies of strange things', the spectral was part of the oriental landscape. Lakes, mountains, ruined castles and terraced fields were the natural locale of ghostly spirits. Hearn's apparitions are not a violent intrusion upon everyday reality;

they are already a part of that reality, co-existing with the living. This is epitomised by the Japanese verse which Hearn included in his volume *In Ghostly Japan*:

> Think not that dreams
>   appear to the dreamer
>   only at night:
> The dream of this world of pain
>   appears to us
>   even by day.

The many nature-spirits, goblins and ghosts who inhabit his stories, can be either benign or malignant. Often part of the tension in the narrative is created by this uncertainty. We have to wait until the end to find out. However, there are some tales such as *Mujina* that just shock you with their inexplicable horror. *Mujina* is in essence just a fragment, a snatched moment; there is no plot. Within this slender tale, told as one would relate an anecdote to a friend, Hearn is able chill you to the marrow and then, cunningly he abandons you with the horrible image fixed in your mind: ' – and the man saw that she had no eyes or nose or mouth – and he screamed . . . '

Similarly in *Jikininki*, the spirit appears as a 'Shape, vague and vast . . . '. It is a shape which devours corpses. This story begins like so many classic ghost-stories, with the weary traveller seeking shelter for the night. The events that follow, told in chilling matter-of-fact details which enhance the horror, are surprising and remarkably cinematic. A *jikininki* is literally a man-eating goblin, surely a candidate to join that notorious pantheon of horror creatures such as vampires, werewolves and zombies.

The Story of Mimi-Nashi-Hoichi is a rare instance where Hearn uses violence to achieve an unsettling effect when the phantom warrior rips the ears from a blind musician's head. The moment occurs so matter-of-factly and without any grand build-up that the moment achieves far greater shock as a result. Nevertheless, the author is not attempting to replicate the violence, gore and savagery of the British horror-tale of the time; he is merely reflecting the acceptance of such behaviour by the people of feudal Japan. He is conscious that the sense of ceremony, love of delicacy and beauty beloved by the oriental sits beside the paradoxical streak of cruelty which is also inherent in the culture. This contrast is effectively captured in the tone and delivery of these stories.

It could be said that *The Story of Mimi-Nashi-Hoichi* uses dramatic shock effects and the broad nightmarish moments of the Kabuki theatre, but in general the author turned his attention to smaller dramas and with these he is capable of subtle effects and stylised moments that reflect the ritualistic grace of the No plays.

The genius of Lafcadio Hearn lies in the telling of the stories rather than the plots, for most of them are tales that he had either heard or read about. In essence he is effectively translating the oriental narratives into an English prose for a Western audience. But he is doing much more than just that. Because of his affinity with the Japanese people and culture, he manages to retain the true oriental 'feel' and nature of the originals. He does this brilliantly: interpreting the Japanese philosophy and social mores so that they become understandable to the Western mind. He was not just concerned with capturing the basic details of the story but expressing the philosophical and psychological traits inherent in these narratives.

One of Hearn's longer pieces is *A Passional Karma*, which, he explains in the opening passages, is his version of a 'weird play', *Peony Lantern*, originally performed on stage in colloquial Japanese, and 'purely Japanese in local color'. In adapting this story for the occidental reader he admits that one of his aims is 'to explain some popular ideas of the supernatural which Western people know very little about.' He adds that the conversational passages, 'happen to possess a particular quality of psychological interest'.

To use his own phrase, Hearn always sought for that elusive quality of 'weird beauty' in his supernatural tales. He strove also for simplicity and delicacy, and avoidance of the contrived and the obvious. In his introduction to *Some Chinese Ghosts*, commenting on style and approach to his stories, he notes that 'I could not forget this striking observation in Sir Walter Scott's *Essay on Imitations of the Ancient Ballad*:

> The supernatural, though appealing to certain powerful emotions very widely and deeply sown amongst the human race is, nevertheless, *a spring which is perfectly apt to lose its elasticity by being too much pressed upon.*

It is a case of take the reader by the hand and lead them into the unknown, rather than thrust them into the darkness.

Another of the great pleasures to be found in reading these tales is in the variety of tone and effect that is achieved. While the stories all fit neatly under that amorphous umbrella of 'ghost and supernatural fiction', some contain elements from other genres. In particular, many have the mood and style of the fairy-story. They are like dark tales as told by Hans Christian Andersen. Take *Yuki-Onna*, for example, which could be re-titled *Woman of the Snow* (in fact it was called this when several of Hearn's stories were filmed in Japan in 1964 in the movie *Kwaidan*).

The opening sentence is pure fairy-story: 'In a village of Musashi, there lived two woodcutters: Mosaku and Minokichi.' There follows a fantastic tale of a snow-deity who metamorphoses into a beautiful woman; secrets, wishes, forgiveness and, in this instance, a fairly happy ending. A harsher dénouement is found in another of these Andersenesque tales – *Oshidori* – which features the callous shooting of a duck and its consequences. The theme of personal responsibility, which is a common element in much of Hearn's work, is featured strongly in this particular tale. The hunter who thoughtlessly killed the duck is filled with remorse by the horrific events that unfold, a remorse which causes him to shave his head and become a priest.

The stories of Lafcadio Hearn in this volume are taken from three of his supernatural collections, *Some Chinese Ghosts* (1887), *In Ghostly Japan* (1899), *Kwaidan* (1904), and they represent the best of his writings in the supernatural field. Sadly today Hearn is a little-known figure in the pantheon of ghost-story/supernatural authors, except by a few cognoscenti who read and study the genre widely. Hopefully, this volume will help to redress the balance and introduce him to a whole new generation of readers. It is true that he is not a roaring fiery force in the world of supernatural literature, rather a subtle and elusive candle-flame gently illuminating some dark and esoteric corners of the oriental consciousness. Nevertheless there is a power and force in his fiction which stays with you long after you finish reading.

It has been observed by several reviewers that Hearn's style echoes the oral traditions of the Japanese folk-tale. Indeed many of his accounts begin in a conversational tone as though the author is speaking directly to the reader in a familiar and friendly fashion. It has also been suggested that Hearn's lean, terse style anticipates the sparse prose of the American author Ernest Hemingway, although differing subject-matter and the tonal differences between the two writers make this comparison a little strained.

However, any academic analysis of Hearn's output is really of little consequence to the avid reader of ghost tales. If you are like me, when you begin reading and enjoying these fascinating short stories full of 'weird beauty' you will find yourself being driven on – to read just one more little gem before putting the book down. Beware, you could end up reading the whole volume in one session!

DAVID STUART DAVIES

KWAIDAN

Stories and Studies
of Strange Things

Most of the following *Kwaidan*, or Weird Tales, have been taken from old Japanese books – such as the *Yaso-Kidan*, *Bukkyo-Hyakkwa-Zensho*, *Kokon-Chomonshu*, *Tama-Sudare*, and *Hyaku-Monogatari*. Some of the stories may have had a Chinese origin: the very remarkable 'Dream of Akinosuke', for example, is certainly from a Chinese source. But the story-teller, in every case, has so recoloured and reshaped his borrowing as to naturalize it . . . One queer tale, 'Yuki-Onna', was told me by a farmer of Chofu, Nishitama-gori, in Musashi province, as a legend of his native village. Whether it has ever been written in Japanese I do not know; but the extraordinary belief which it records used certainly to exist in most parts of Japan, and in many curious forms . . . The incident of 'Riki-Baka' was a personal experience; and I wrote it down almost exactly as it happened, changing only a family-name mentioned by the Japanese narrator.

L.H.
Tokyo, Japan
January 20th, 1904

THE STORY OF MIMI-NASHI-HOÏCHI

The Story of Mimi-nashi-Hoïchi

More than seven hundred years ago, at Dan-no-ura, in the Straits of Shimonoseki, was fought the last battle of the long contest between the Heike, or Taira clan, and the Genji, or Minamoto clan. There the Heike perished utterly, with their women and children, and their infant emperor likewise – now remembered as Antoku Tenno. And that sea and shore have been haunted for seven hundred years . . . Elsewhere I told you about the strange crabs found there, called Heike crabs, which have human faces on their backs, and are said to be the spirits of the Heike warriors.[1] But there are many strange things to be seen and heard along that coast. On dark nights thousands of ghostly fires hover about the beach, or flit above the waves – pale lights which the fishermen call *Oni-bi*, or demon-fires; and, whenever the winds are up, a sound of great shouting comes from that sea, like a clamour of battle.

In former years the Heike were much more restless than they now are. They would rise about ships passing in the night, and try to sink them; and at all times they would watch for swimmers, to pull them down. It was in order to appease those dead that the Buddhist temple, Amidaji, was built at Akamagaseki.[2] A cemetery also was made close by, near the beach; and within it were set up monuments inscribed with the names of the drowned emperor and of his great vassals; and Buddhist services were regularly performed there, on behalf of the spirits of them. After the temple had been built, and the tombs erected, the Heike gave less trouble than before; but they continued to do queer things at intervals – proving that they had not found the perfect peace.

Some centuries ago there lived at Akamagaseki a blind man named Hoïchi, who was famed for his skill in recitation and in playing upon

1 See my *Kotto*, for a description of these curious crabs.
2 Or, Shimonoseki. The town is also known by the name of Bakkan.

the *biwa*.[1] From childhood he had been trained to recite and to play;
and while yet a lad he had surpassed his teachers. As a professional
biwa-hoshi he became famous chiefly by his recitations of the history
of the Heike and the Genji; and it is said that when he sang the song
of the battle of Dan-no-ura 'even the goblins [*kijin*] could not refrain
from tears.'

At the outset of his career, Hoïchi was very poor; but he found
a good friend to help him. The priest of the Amidaji was fond
of poetry and music; and he often invited Hoïchi to the temple,
to play and recite. Afterwards, being much impressed by the wonderful skill of the lad, the priest proposed that Hoïchi should
make the temple his home; and this offer was gratefully accepted.
Hoïchi was given a room in the temple-building; and, in return
for food and lodging, he was required only to gratify the priest
with a musical performance on certain evenings, when otherwise
disengaged.

One summer night the priest was called away, to perform a Buddhist
service at the house of a dead parishioner; and he went there with his
acolyte, leaving Hoïchi alone in the temple. It was a hot night; and
the blind man sought to cool himself on the verandah before his
sleeping-room. The verandah overlooked a small garden in the rear
of the Amidaji. There Hoïchi waited for the priest's return, and tried
to relieve his solitude by practising upon his *biwa*. Midnight passed;
and the priest did not appear. But the atmosphere was still too warm
for comfort within doors; and Hoïchi remained outside. At last he
heard steps approaching from the back gate. Somebody crossed the
garden, advanced to the verandah, and halted directly in front of
him – but it was not the priest. A deep voice called the blind man's
name – abruptly and unceremoniously, in the manner of a samurai
summoning an inferior: 'Hoïchi!'

'*Hai*!'[2] answered the blind man, frightened by the menace in the
voice – 'I am blind! – I cannot know who calls!'

---

1 The *biwa*, a kind of four-stringed lute, is chiefly used in musical recitative.
Formerly the professional minstrels who recited the *Heike-Monogatari*, and other
tragical histories, were called *biwa-hoshi*, or 'lute-priests'. The origin of this
appellation is not clear; but it is possible that it may have been suggested by the
fact that 'lute-priests' as well as blind shampooers, had their heads shaven, like
Buddhist priests. The *biwa* is played with a kind of plectrum, called *bachi*, usually
made of horn.
2 A response to show that one has heard and is listening attentively.

'There is nothing to fear,' the stranger exclaimed, speaking more gently. 'I am stopping near this temple, and have been sent to you with a message. My present lord, a person of exceedingly high rank, is now staying in Akamagaseki, with many noble attendants. He wished to view the scene of the battle of Dan-no-ura; and today he visited that place. Having heard of your skill in reciting the story of the battle, he now desires to hear your performance: so you will take your *biwa* and come with me at once to the house where the august assembly is waiting.'

In those times, the order of a samurai was not to be lightly disobeyed. Hoïchi donned his sandals, took his *biwa*, and went away with the stranger, who guided him deftly, but obliged him to walk very fast. The hand that guided was iron; and the clank of the warrior's stride proved him fully armed – probably some palace-guard on duty. Hoïchi's first alarm was over: he began to imagine himself in good luck – for, remembering the retainer's assurance about a 'person of exceedingly high rank', he thought that the lord who wished to hear the recitation could not be less than a daimyo of the first class. Presently the samurai halted; and Hoïchi became aware that they had arrived at a large gateway – and he wondered, for he could not remember any large gate in that part of the town, except the main gate of the Amidaji. '*Kaimon!*' [1] the samurai called – and there was a sound of unbarring; and the twain passed on. They traversed a space of garden, and halted again before some entrance; and the retainer cried in a loud voice, 'Within there! I have brought Hoïchi.' Then came sounds of feet hurrying, and screens sliding, and rain-doors opening, and voices of women in converse. By the language of the women Hoïchi knew them to be domestics in some noble household; but he could not imagine to what place he had been conducted. Little time was allowed him for conjecture. After he had been helped to mount several stone steps, upon the last of which he was told to leave his sandals, a woman's hand guided him along interminable reaches of polished planking, and round pillared angles too many to remember, and over widths amazing of matted floor – into the middle of some vast apartment. There he thought that many great people were assembled: the sound of the rustling of silk was like the sound of leaves in a forest. He heard also a great humming of voices – talking in undertones; and the speech was the speech of courts.

1 A respectful term, signifying the opening of a gate. It was used by samurai when calling to the guards on duty at a lord's gate for admission.

Hoïchi was told to put himself at ease, and he found a kneeling-cushion ready for him. After having taken his place upon it, and tuned his instrument, the voice of a woman – whom he divined to be the *Rojo*, or matron in charge of the female service – addressed him, saying: 'It is now required that the history of the Heike be recited, to the accompaniment of the *biwa*.'

Now the entire recital would have required a time of many nights; therefore Hoïchi ventured a question: 'As the whole of the story is not soon told, what portion is it augustly desired that I now recite?'

The woman's voice made answer: 'Recite the story of the battle at Dan-no-ura – for the pity of it is the most deep.'[1]

Then Hoïchi lifted up his voice, and chanted the chant of the fight on the bitter sea – wonderfully making his *biwa* to sound like the straining of oars and the rushing of ships, the whirr and the hissing of arrows, the shouting and trampling of men, the crashing of steel upon helmets, the plunging of slain in the flood. And to left and right of him, in the pauses of his playing, he could hear voices murmuring praise: 'How marvellous an artist!' – 'Never in our own province was playing heard like this!' – 'Not in all the empire is there another singer like Hoïchi!' Then fresh courage came to him, and he played and sang yet better than before; and a hush of wonder deepened about him. But when at last he came to tell the fate of the fair and helpless – the piteous perishing of the women and children – and the death-leap of Nii-no-Ama, with the imperial infant in her arms – then all the listeners uttered together one long, long shuddering cry of anguish; and thereafter they wept and wailed so loudly and so wildly that the blind man was frightened by the violence and grief that he had made. For much time the sobbing and the wailing continued. But gradually the sounds of lamentation died away; and again, in the great stillness that followed, Hoïchi heard the voice of the woman whom he supposed to be the *Rojo*.

She said: 'Although we had been assured that you were a very skilful player upon the *biwa*, and without an equal in recitative, we did not know that any one could be so skilful as you have proved yourself tonight. Our lord has been pleased to say that he intends to bestow upon you a fitting reward. But he desires that you shall perform before him once every night for the next six nights – after which time he will probably make his august return-journey.

1 Or the phrase might be rendered, 'for the pity of that part is the deepest.' The Japanese word for pity in the original text is *aware*.

Tomorrow night, therefore, you are to come here at the same hour. The retainer who tonight conducted you will be sent for you . . . There is another matter about which I have been ordered to inform you. It is required that you shall speak to no-one of your visits here, during the time of our lord's august sojourn at Akamagaseki. As he is travelling incognito,[1] he commands that no mention of these things be made . . . You are now free to go back to your temple.'

After Hoïchi had duly expressed his thanks, a woman's hand conducted him to the entrance of the house, where the same retainer who had before guided him, was waiting to take him home. The retainer led him to the verandah at the rear of the temple, and there bade him farewell.

It was almost dawn when Hoïchi returned; but his absence from the temple had not been observed – as the priest, coming back at a very late hour, had supposed him asleep. During the day Hoïchi was able to take some rest; and he said nothing about his strange adventure. In the middle of the following night the samurai again came for him, and led him to the august assembly, where he gave another recitation with the same success that had attended his previous performance. But during this second visit his absence from the temple was accidentally discovered; and after his return in the morning he was summoned to the presence of the priest, who said to him, in a tone of kindly reproach: 'We have been very anxious about you, friend Hoïchi. To go out, blind and alone, at so late an hour, is dangerous. Why did you go without telling us? I could have ordered a servant to accompany you. And where have you been?'

Hoïchi answered, evasively: 'Pardon me kind friend! I had to attend to some private business; and I could not arrange the matter at any other hour.'

The priest was surprised, rather than pained, by Hoïchi's reticence: he felt it to be unnatural, and suspected something wrong. He feared that the blind lad had been bewitched or deluded by some evil spirits. He did not ask any more questions; but he privately instructed the men-servants of the temple to keep watch upon Hoïchi's movements, and to follow him in case that he should again leave the temple after dark.

---

1 'Travelling incognito' is at least the meaning of the original phrase – 'making a disguised august-journey' (*shinobi no go-ryoko*).

On the very next night, Hoïchi was seen to leave the temple; and the servants immediately lighted their lanterns, and followed after him. But it was a rainy night, and very dark; and before the temple-folks could get to the roadway, Hoïchi had disappeared. Evidently he had walked very fast – a strange thing, considering his blindness; for the road was in a bad condition. The men hurried through the streets, making inquiries at every house which Hoïchi was accustomed to visit; but nobody could give them any news of him. At last, as they were returning to the temple by way of the shore, they were startled by the sound of a *biwa*, furiously played, in the cemetery of the Amidaji. Except for some ghostly fires – such as usually flitted there on dark nights – all was blackness in that direction. But the men at once hastened to the cemetery; and there, by the help of their lanterns, they discovered Hoïchi – sitting alone in the rain before the memorial tomb of Antoku Tenno, making his *biwa* resound, and loudly chanting the chant of the battle of Dan-no-ura. And behind him, and about him, and everywhere above the tombs, the fires of the dead were burning, like candles. Never before had so great a host of *Oni-bi* appeared in the sight of mortal man . . .

'Hoïchi San! – Hoïchi San!' the servants cried – 'you are be-witched! . . . Hoïchi San!'

But the blind man did not seem to hear. Strenuously he made his *biwa* to rattle and ring and clang – more and more wildly he chanted the chant of the battle of Dan-no-ura. They caught hold of him – they shouted into his ear: 'Hoïchi San! – Hoïchi San! – come home with us at once!'

Reprovingly he spoke to them: 'To interrupt me in such a manner, before this august assembly, will not be tolerated.'

Whereat, in spite of the weirdness of the thing, the servants could not help laughing. Sure that he had been bewitched, they now seized him, and pulled him up on his feet, and by main force hurried him back to the temple – where he was immediately relieved of his wet clothes, by order of the priest. Then the priest insisted upon a full explanation of his friend's astonishing behaviour.

Hoïchi long hesitated to speak. But at last, finding that his con-duct had really alarmed and angered the good priest, he decided to abandon his reserve; and he related everything that had happened from the time of first visit of the samurai.

The priest said: 'Hoïchi, my poor friend, you are now in great danger! How unfortunate that you did not tell me all this before!

Your wonderful skill in music has indeed brought you into strange trouble. By this time you must be aware that you have not been visiting any house whatever, but have been passing your nights in the cemetery, among the tombs of the Heike – and it was before the memorial-tomb of Antoku Tenno that our people tonight found you, sitting in the rain. All that you have been imagining was illusion – except the calling of the dead. By once obeying them, you have put yourself in their power. If you obey them again, after what has already occurred, they will tear you in pieces. But they would have destroyed you, sooner or later, in any event . . . Now I shall not be able to remain with you tonight: I am called away to perform another service. But, before I go, it will be necessary to protect your body by writing holy texts upon it.'

Before sundown the priest and his acolyte stripped Hoïchi: then, with their writing-brushes, they traced upon his breast and back, head and face and neck, limbs and hands and feet – even upon the soles of his feet, and upon all parts of his body – the text of the holy sutra called *Hannya-Shin-Kyo*.[1] When this had been done, the priest instructed Hoïchi, saying: 'Tonight, as soon as I go away, you must seat yourself on the verandah, and wait. You will be called. But, whatever may happen, do not answer, and do not move. Say nothing and sit still – as if meditating. If you stir, or make any noise, you will be torn asunder. Do not get frightened; and do not think of calling for help – because no help could save you. If you do exactly as I tell you, the danger will pass, and you will have nothing more to fear.'

After dark the priest and the acolyte went away; and Hoïchi seated himself on the verandah, according to the instructions given him. He

1 The Smaller Pragna-Paramita-Hridaya-Sutra is thus called in Japanese. Both the smaller and larger sutras called Pragna-Paramita ('Transcendent Wisdom') have been translated by the late Professor Max Muller, and can be found in volume xlix of the *Sacred Books of the East* ('Buddhist Mahayana Sutras'). – Apropos of the magical use of the text, as described in this story, it is worth remarking that the subject of the sutra is the Doctrine of the Emptiness of Forms – that is to say, of the unreal character of all phenomena or noumena . . . 'Form is emptiness; and emptiness is form. Emptiness is not different from form; form is not different from emptiness. What is form – that is emptiness. What is emptiness – that is form . . . Perception, name, concept, and knowledge, are also emptiness . . . There is no eye, ear, nose, tongue, body, and mind . . . But when the envelopment of consciousness has been annihilated, then he [*the seeker*] becomes free from all fear, and beyond the reach of change, enjoying final Nirvana.'

laid his *biwa* on the planking beside him, and, assuming the attitude
of meditation, remained quite still – taking care not to cough, or to
breathe audibly. For hours he stayed thus.

Then, from the roadway, he heard the steps coming. They passed
the gate, crossed the garden, approached the verandah, stopped –
directly in front of him.

'Hoïchi!' the deep voice called. But the blind man held his breath,
and sat motionless.

'Hoïchi!' grimly called the voice a second time. Then a third
time – savagely: 'Hoïchi!'

Hoïchi remained as still as a stone – and the voice grumbled: 'No
answer! – That won't do! . . . Must see where the fellow is . . . '

There was a noise of heavy feet mounting upon the verandah. The
feet approached deliberately – halted beside him. Then, for long
minutes – during which Hoïchi felt his whole body shake to the
beating of his heart – there was dead silence.

At last the gruff voice muttered close to him: 'Here is the *biwa*; but
of the *biwa*-player I see – only two ears! . . . So that explains why he
did not answer: he had no mouth to answer with – there is nothing
left of him but his ears . . . Now to my lord those ears I will take –
in proof that the august commands have been obeyed, so far as was
possible' . . .

At that instant Hoïchi felt his ears gripped by fingers of iron, and
torn off! Great as the pain was, he gave no cry. The heavy footfalls
receded along the verandah – descended into the garden – passed out
to the roadway – ceased. From either side of his head, the blind man
felt a thick warm trickling; but he dared not lift his hands . . .

Before sunrise the priest came back. He hastened at once to the
verandah in the rear, stepped and slipped upon something clammy,
and uttered a cry of horror – for he saw, by the light of his lantern,
that the clamminess was blood. But he perceived Hoïchi sitting
there, in the attitude of meditation – with the blood still oozing from
his wounds.

'My poor Hoïchi!' cried the startled priest – 'What is this? . . . You
have been hurt?'

At the sound of his friend's voice, the blind man felt safe. He burst
out sobbing, and tearfully told his adventure of the night.

'Poor, poor Hoïchi!' the priest exclaimed – 'all my fault! – My very
grievous fault! . . . Everywhere upon your body the holy texts had
been written – except upon your ears! I trusted my acolyte to do

that part of the work; and it was very, very wrong of me not to have made sure that he had done it! . . . Well, the matter cannot now be helped – we can only try to heal your hurts as soon as possible . . . Cheer up, friend! – the danger is now well over. You will never again be troubled by those visitors.'

With the aid of a good doctor, Hoïchi soon recovered from his injuries. The story of his strange adventure spread far and wide, and soon made him famous. Many noble persons went to Akamagaseki to hear him recite; and large presents of money were given to him – so that he became a wealthy man . . . But from the time of his adventure, he was known only by the appellation of *Mimi-nashi-Hoïchi*: 'Hoïchi-the-Earless'.

OSHIDORI

Oshidori

There was a falconer and hunter, named Sonjo, who lived in the district called Tamura-no-Go, of the province of Mutsu. One day he went out hunting, and could not find any game. But on his way home, at a place called Akanuma, he perceived a pair of *oshidori* [1] (mandarin-ducks), swimming together in a river that he was about to cross. to kill *oshidori* is not good; but Sonjo happened to be very hungry, and he shot at the pair. His arrow pierced the male: the female escaped into the rushes of the further shore, and disappeared. Sonjo took the dead bird home, and cooked it.

That night he dreamed a dreary dream. It seemed to him that a beautiful woman came into his room, and stood by his pillow, and began to weep. So bitterly did she weep that Sonjo felt as if his heart were being torn out while he listened. And the woman cried to him: 'Why – oh! why did you kill him? – Of what wrong was he guilty? . . . At Akanuma we were so happy together – and you killed him! . . . What harm did he ever do you? Do you even know what you have done? – Oh! do you know what a cruel, what a wicked thing you have done? . . . Me too you have killed – for I will not live without my husband! . . . Only to tell you this I came . . . ' Then again she wept aloud – so bitterly that the voice of her crying pierced into the marrow of the listener's bones – and she sobbed out the words of this poem:

> *Hi kurureba*
> *Sasoeshi mono wo –*
> *Akanuma no*
> *Makomo no kure no*
> *Hitori-ne zo uki!*

> [At the coming of twilight
>   I invited him to return with me – !

1 From ancient time, in the Far East, these birds have been regarded as emblems of conjugal affection.

Now to sleep alone
>   in the shadow of the rushes of Akanuma –
Ah! what misery unspeakable!] [1]

And after having uttered these verses she exclaimed: 'Ah, you do not know – you cannot know what you have done! But tomorrow, when you go to Akanuma, you will see – you will see . . . ' So saying, and weeping very piteously, she went away.

When Sonjo awoke in the morning, this dream remained so vivid in his mind that he was greatly troubled. He remembered the words: 'But tomorrow, when you go to Akanuma, you will see – you will see.' And he resolved to go there at once, that he might learn whether his dream was anything more than a dream.

So he went to Akanuma; and there, when he came to the river-bank, he saw the female *oshidori* swimming alone. In the same moment the bird perceived Sonjo; but, instead of trying to escape, she swam straight towards him, looking at him the while in a strange fixed way. Then, with her beak, she suddenly tore open her own body, and died before the hunter's eyes . . .

Sonjo shaved his head, and became a priest.

[1] There is a pathetic double meaning in the third verse; for the syllables composing the proper name *Akanuma* ('Red Marsh') may also be read as *akanu-ma*, signifying 'the time of our inseparable (or delightful) relation'. So the poem can also be thus rendered: 'When the day began to fail, I had invited him to accompany me . . . ! Now, after the time of that happy relation, what misery for the one who must slumber alone in the shadow of the rushes!' – The *makomo* is a short of large rush, used for making baskets.

THE STORY OF O-TEI

The Story of O-Tei

A long time ago, in the town of Niigata, in the province of Echizen, there lived a man called Nagao Chosei.

Nagao was the son of a physician, and was educated for his father's profession. At an early age he had been betrothed to a girl called O-Tei, the daughter of one of his father's friends; and both families had agreed that the wedding should take place as soon as Nagao had finished his studies. But the health of O-Tei proved to be weak; and in her fifteenth year she was attacked by a fatal consumption. When she became aware that she must die, she sent for Nagao to bid him farewell.

As he knelt at her bedside, she said to him: 'Nagao-Sama,[1] my betrothed, we were promised to each other from the time of our childhood; and we were to have been married at the end of this year. But now I am going to die – the gods know what is best for us. If I were able to live for some years longer, I could only continue to be a cause of trouble and grief for others. With this frail body, I could not be a good wife; and therefore even to wish to live, for your sake, would be a very selfish wish. I am quite resigned to die; and I want you to promise that you will not grieve . . . Besides, I want to tell you that I think we shall meet again . . . '

'Indeed we shall meet again,' Nagao answered earnestly. 'And in that Pure Land[2] there will be no pain of separation.'

'Nay, nay!' she responded softly, 'I meant not the Pure Land. I believe that we are destined to meet again in this world – although I shall be buried tomorrow.'

Nagao looked at her wonderingly, and saw her smile at his wonder. She continued, in her gentle, dreamy voice: 'Yes, I mean in this world – in your own present life, Nagao-Sama . . . Providing, indeed, that you wish it. Only, for this thing to happen, I must again be born a girl, and grow up to womanhood. So you would have to wait.

1 '-sama' is a polite suffix attached to personal names.
2 A Buddhist term commonly used to signify a kind of heaven.

Fifteen – sixteen years: that is a long time . . . But, my promised husband, you are now only nineteen years old . . .'

Eager to soothe her dying moments, he answered tenderly: 'To wait for you, my betrothed, were no less a joy than a duty. We are pledged to each other for the time of seven existences.'

'But you doubt?' she questioned, watching his face.

'My dear one,' he answered, 'I doubt whether I should be able to know you in another body, under another name – unless you can tell me of a sign or token.'

'That I cannot do,' she said. 'Only the Gods and the Buddhas know how and where we shall meet. But I am sure – very, very sure – that, if you be not unwilling to receive me, I shall be able to come back to you . . . Remember these words of mine . . .'

She ceased to speak; and her eyes closed. She was dead.

* * *

Nagao had been sincerely attached to O-Tei; and his grief was deep. He had a mortuary tablet made, inscribed with her *zokumyo*;[1] and he placed the tablet in his *butsudan*,[2] and every day set offerings before it. He thought a great deal about the strange things that O-Tei had said to him just before her death; and, in the hope of pleasing her spirit, he wrote a solemn promise to wed her if she could ever return to him in another body. This written promise he sealed with his seal, and placed in the *butsudan* beside the mortuary tablet of O-Tei.

Nevertheless, as Nagao was an only son, it was necessary that he should marry. He soon found himself obliged to yield to the wishes of his family, and to accept a wife of his father's choosing. After his marriage he continued to set offerings before the tablet of O-Tei; and he never failed to remember her with affection. But by degrees her image became dim in his memory – like a dream that is hard to recall. And the years went by.

During those years many misfortunes came upon him. He lost his parents by death – then his wife and his only child. So that he found himself alone in the world. He abandoned his desolate home, and set out upon a long journey in the hope of forgetting his sorrows.

1 The Buddhist term *zokumyo* ('profane name') signifies the personal name, borne during life, in contradistinction to the *kaimyo* ('sila-name') or *homyo* ('law-name') given after death – religious posthumous appellations inscribed upon the tomb, and upon the mortuary tablet in the parish-temple. – For some account of these, see my paper entitled 'The Literature of the Dead', in *Exotics and Retrospectives*.
2 Buddhist household shrine.

One day, in the course of his travels, he arrived at Ikao – a mountain-village still famed for its thermal springs, and for the beautiful scenery of its neighbourhood. In the village-inn at which he stopped, a young girl came to wait upon him; and, at the first sight of her face, he felt his heart leap as it had never leaped before. So strangely did she resemble O-Tei that he pinched himself to make sure that he was not dreaming. As she went and came – bringing fire and food, or arranging the chamber of the guest – her every attitude and motion revived in him some gracious memory of the girl to whom he had been pledged in his youth. He spoke to her; and she responded in a soft, clear voice of which the sweetness saddened him with a sadness of other days.

Then, in great wonder, he questioned her, saying: 'Elder Sister,[1] so much do you look like a person whom I knew long ago, that I was startled when you first entered this room. Pardon me, therefore, for asking what is your native place, and what is your name?'

Immediately – and in the unforgotten voice of the dead – she thus made answer: 'My name is O-Tei; and you are Nagao Chosei of Echigo, my promised husband. Seventeen years ago, I died in Niigata: then you made in writing a promise to marry me if ever I could come back to this world in the body of a woman – and you sealed that written promise with your seal, and put it in the *butsudan*, beside the tablet inscribed with my name. And therefore I came back . . . '

As she uttered these last words, she fell unconscious.

Nagao married her; and the marriage was a happy one. But at no time afterwards could she remember what she had told him in answer to his question at Ikao: neither could she remember anything of her previous existence. The recollection of the former birth – mysteriously kindled in the moment of that meeting – had again become obscured, and so thereafter remained.

1 Direct translation of a Japanese form of address used toward young, unmarried women.

UBAZAKURA

Ubazakura

Three hundred years ago, in the village called Asamimura, in the district called Onsengori, in the province of Iyo, there lived a good man named Tokubei. This Tokubei was the richest person in the district, and the *muraosa*, or headman, of the village. In most matters he was fortunate; but he reached the age of forty without knowing the happiness of becoming a father. Therefore he and his wife, in the affliction of their childlessness, addressed many prayers to the divinity Fudo Myo O, who had a famous temple, called Saihoji, in Asamimura.

At last their prayers were heard: the wife of Tokubei gave birth to a daughter. The child was very pretty; and she received the name of Tsuyu. As the mother's milk was deficient, a milk-nurse, called O-Sode, was hired for the little one.

O-Tsuyu grew up to be a very beautiful girl; but at the age of fifteen she fell sick, and the doctors thought that she was going to die. In that time the nurse O-Sode, who loved O-Tsuyu with a real mother's love, went to the temple Saihoji, and fervently prayed to Fudo-Sama on behalf of the girl. Every day, for twenty-one days, she went to the temple and prayed; and at the end of that time, O-Tsuyu suddenly and completely recovered.

Then there was great rejoicing in the house of Tokubei; and he gave a feast to all his friends in celebration of the happy event. But on the night of the feast the nurse O-Sode was suddenly taken ill; and on the following morning, the doctor, who had been summoned to attend her, announced that she was dying.

Then the family, in great sorrow, gathered about her bed, to bid her farewell. But she said to them: 'It is time that I should tell you something which you do not know. My prayer has been heard. I besought Fudo-Sama that I might be permitted to die in the place of O-Tsuyu; and this great favour has been granted me. Therefore you must not grieve about my death ... But I have one request to make.

I promised Fudo-Sama that I would have a cherry-tree planted in the garden of Saihoji, for a thank-offering and a commemoration. Now I shall not be able myself to plant the tree there: so I must beg that you will fulfil that vow for me . . . Good-bye, dear friends; and remember that I was happy to die for O-Tsuyu's sake.'

After the funeral of O-Sode, a young cherry-tree – the finest that could be found – was planted in the garden of Saihoji by the parents of O-Tsuyu. The tree grew and flourished; and on the sixteenth day of the second month of the following year – the anniversary of O-Sode's death – it blossomed in a wonderful way. So it continued to blossom for two hundred and fifty-four years – always upon the sixteenth day of the second month – and its flowers, pink and white, were like the nipples of a woman's breasts, bedewed with milk. And the people called it *Ubazakura*, the Cherry-tree of the Milk-Nurse.

DIPLOMACY

Diplomacy

It had been ordered that the execution should take place in the garden of the *yashiki*.[1] So the man was taken there, and made to kneel down in a wide sanded space crossed by a line of *tobi-ishi*, or stepping-stones, such as you may still see in Japanese landscape-gardens. His arms were bound behind him. Retainers brought water in buckets, and rice-bags filled with pebbles; and they packed the rice-bags round the kneeling man – so wedging him in that he could not move.

The master came, and observed the arrangements. He found them satisfactory, and made no remarks.

Suddenly the condemned man cried out to him: 'Honoured Sir, the fault for which I have been doomed I did not wittingly commit. It was only my very great stupidity which caused the fault. Having been born stupid, by reason of my Karma, I could not always help making mistakes. But to kill a man for being stupid is wrong – and that wrong will be repaid. So surely as you kill me, so surely shall I be avenged – out of the resentment that you provoke will come the vengeance; and evil will be rendered for evil . . .'

If any person be killed while feeling strong resentment, the ghost of that person will be able to take vengeance upon the killer. This the samurai knew. He replied very gently – almost caressingly: 'We shall allow you to frighten us as much as you please – after you are dead. But it is difficult to believe that you mean what you say. Will you try to give us some sign of your great resentment – after your head has been cut off?'

'Assuredly I will,' answered the man.

'Very well,' said the samurai, drawing his long sword – 'I am now going to cut off your head. Directly in front of you there is a stepping-stone. After your head has been cut off, try to bite the stepping-stone. If your angry ghost can help you to do that, some of us may be frightened . . . Will you try to bite the stone?'

1 The spacious house and grounds of a wealthy person is thus called.

'I will bite it!' cried the man, in great anger – 'I will bite it! – I will bite – '

There was a flash, a swish, a crunching thud: the bound body bowed over the rice sacks – two long blood-jets pumping from the shorn neck – and the head rolled upon the sand. Heavily toward the stepping-stone it rolled: then, suddenly bounding, it caught the upper edge of the stone between its teeth, clung desperately for a moment, and dropped inert.

None spoke; but the retainers stared in horror at their master. He seemed to be quite unconcerned. He merely held out his sword to the nearest attendant, who, with a wooden dipper, poured water over the blade from haft to point, and then carefully wiped the steel several times with sheets of soft paper . . . And thus ended the ceremonial part of the incident.

For months thereafter, the retainers and the domestics lived in ceaseless fear of ghostly visitation. None of them doubted that the promised vengeance would come; and their constant terror caused them to hear and to see much that did not exist. They became afraid of the sound of the wind in the bamboos – afraid even of the stirring of shadows in the garden. At last, after taking counsel together, they decided to petition their master to have a *Segaki*-service [1] performed on behalf of the vengeful spirit.

'Quite unnecessary,' the samurai said, when his chief retainer had uttered the general wish . . . 'I understand that the desire of a dying man for revenge may be a cause for fear. But in this case there is nothing to fear.'

The retainer looked at his master beseechingly, but hesitated to ask the reason of the alarming confidence.

'Oh, the reason is simple enough,' declared the samurai, divining the unspoken doubt. 'Only the very last intention of the fellow could have been dangerous; and when I challenged him to give me the sign, I diverted his mind from the desire of revenge. He died with the set purpose of biting the stepping-stone; and that purpose he was able to accomplish, but nothing else. All the rest he must have forgotten . . . So you need not feel any further anxiety about the matter.'

– And indeed the dead man gave no more trouble. Nothing at all happened.

1　A Buddhist service for the dead.

OF A MIRROR AND A BELL

Of a Mirror and a Bell

Eight centuries ago, the priests of Mugenyama, in the province of Totomi,[1] wanted a big bell for their temple; and they asked the women of their parish to help them by contributing old bronze mirrors for bell-metal.

[Even today, in the courts of certain Japanese temples, you may see heaps of old bronze mirrors contributed for such a purpose. The largest collection of this kind that I ever saw was in the court of a temple of the Jodo sect, at Hakata, in Kyushu: the mirrors had been given for the making of a bronze statue of Amida, thirty-three feet high.]

There was at that time a young woman, a farmer's wife, living at Mugenyama, who presented her mirror to the temple, to be used for bell-metal. But afterwards she much regretted her mirror. She remembered things that her mother had told her about it; and she remembered that it had belonged, not only to her mother but to her mother's mother and grandmother; and she remembered some happy smiles which it had reflected. Of course, if she could have offered the priests a certain sum of money in place of the mirror, she could have asked them to give back her heirloom. But she had not the money necessary. Whenever she went to the temple, she saw her mirror lying in the court-yard, behind a railing, among hundreds of other mirrors heaped there together. She knew it by the *Sho-Chiku-Bai* in relief on the back of it – those three fortunate emblems of Pine, Bamboo, and Plumflower, which delighted her baby eyes when her mother first showed her the mirror. She longed for some chance to steal the mirror, and hide it – that she might thereafter treasure it always. But the chance did not come; and she became very unhappy – felt as if she had foolishly given away a part of her life. She thought about the old saying that a mirror is the Soul of a Woman – (a saying mystically expressed, by the Chinese character for Soul,

1 Part of present-day Shizuoka Prefecture.

upon the backs of many bronze mirrors) – and she feared that it was true in weirder ways than she had before imagined. But she could not dare to speak of her pain to anybody.

Now, when all the mirrors contributed for the Mugenyama bell had been sent to the foundry, the bell-founders discovered that there was one mirror among them which would not melt. Again and again they tried to melt it; but it resisted all their efforts. Evidently the woman who had given that mirror to the temple must have regretted the giving. She had not presented her offering with all her heart; and therefore her selfish soul, remaining attached to the mirror, kept it hard and cold in the midst of the furnace.

Of course everybody heard of the matter, and everybody soon knew whose mirror it was that would not melt. And because of this public exposure of her secret fault, the poor woman became very much ashamed and very angry. And as she could not bear the shame, she drowned herself, after having written a farewell letter containing these words:

> *When I am dead, it will not be difficult to melt the mirror and to cast the bell. But, to the person who breaks that bell by ringing it, great wealth will be given by the ghost of me.*

– You must know that the last wish or promise of anybody who dies in anger, or performs suicide in anger, is generally supposed to possess a supernatural force. After the dead woman's mirror had been melted, and the bell had been successfully cast, people remembered the words of that letter. They felt sure that the spirit of the writer would give wealth to the breaker of the bell; and, as soon as the bell had been suspended in the court of the temple, they went in multitude to ring it. With all their might and main they swung the ringing-beam; but the bell proved to be a good bell, and it bravely withstood their assaults. Nevertheless, the people were not easily discouraged. Day after day, at all hours, they continued to ring the bell furiously – caring nothing whatever for the protests of the priests. So the ringing became an affliction; and the priests could not endure it; and they got rid of the bell by rolling it down the hill into a swamp. The swamp was deep, and swallowed it up – and that was the end of the bell. Only its legend remains; and in that legend it is called the *Mugen-Kane*, or Bell of Mugen.

*   *   *

Now there are queer old Japanese beliefs in the magical efficacy of a certain mental operation implied, though not described, by the verb *nazoraeru*. The word itself cannot be adequately rendered by any English word; for it is used in relation to many kinds of mimetic magic, as well as in relation to the performance of many religious acts of faith. Common meanings of *nazoraeru*, according to dictionaries, are 'to imitate', 'to compare', 'to liken'; but the esoteric meaning is *to substitute, in imagination, one object or action for another, so as to bring about some magical or miraculous result*.

For example – you cannot afford to build a Buddhist temple; but you can easily lay a pebble before the image of the Buddha, with the same pious feeling that would prompt you to build a temple if you were rich enough to build one. The merit of so offering the pebble becomes equal, or almost equal, to the merit of erecting a temple . . . You cannot read the six thousand seven hundred and seventy-one volumes of the Buddhist texts; but you can make a revolving library, containing them, turn round, by pushing it like a windlass; and if you push with an earnest wish that you could read the six thousand seven hundred and seventy-one volumes, you will acquire the same merit as the reading of them would enable you to gain . . . So much will perhaps suffice to explain the religious meanings of *nazoraeru*.

The magical meanings could not all be explained without a great variety of examples; but, for present purposes, the following will serve. If you should make a little man of straw, for the same reason that Sister Helen made a little man of wax – and nail it, with nails not less than five inches long, to some tree in a temple-grove at the Hour of the Ox[1] – and if the person, imaginatively represented by that little straw man, should die thereafter in atrocious agony – that would illustrate one signification of *nazoraeru* . . . Or, let us suppose that a robber has entered your house during the night, and carried away your valuables. If you can discover the footprints of that robber in your garden, and then promptly burn a very large *moxa* on each of them, the soles of the feet of the robber will become inflamed, and will allow him no rest until he returns, of his own accord, to put himself at your mercy. That is another kind of mimetic magic expressed by the term *nazoraeru*. And a third kind is illustrated by various legends of the *Mugen-Kane*.

[1] The two-hour period between 1 a.m. and 3 a.m.

After the bell had been rolled into the swamp, there was, of course, no more chance of ringing it in such wise as to break it. But persons who regretted this loss of opportunity would strike and break objects imaginatively substituted for the bell – thus hoping to please the spirit of the owner of the mirror that had made so much trouble. One of these persons was a woman called Umegae – famed in Japanese legend because of her relation to Kajiwara Kagesue, a warrior of the Heike clan. While the pair were travelling together, Kajiwara one day found himself in great straits for want of money; and Umegae, remembering the tradition of the Bell of Mugen, took a basin of bronze, and, mentally representing it to be the bell, beat upon it until she broke it – crying out, at the same time, for three hundred pieces of gold. A guest of the inn where the pair were stopping made enquiry as to the cause of the banging and the crying, and, on learning the story of the trouble, actually presented Umegae with three hundred *ryo* [1] in gold. Afterwards a song was made about Umegae's basin of bronze; and that song is sung by dancing girls even to this day:

> *Umegae no chozubachi tataite*
> *O-kane ga deru naraba*
> *Mina San mi-uke wo*
> *Sore tanomimasu*

[If, by striking upon the wash-basin of Umegae,
  I could make honourable money come to me,
    then would I negotiate for the freedom
      of all my girl-comrades.]

After this happening, the fame of the *Mugen-Kane* became great; and many people followed the example of Umegae – thereby hoping to emulate her luck. Among these folk was a dissolute farmer who lived near Mugenyama, on the bank of the Oigawa. Having wasted his substance in riotous living, this farmer made for himself, out of the mud in his garden, a clay model of the *Mugen-Kane*; and he beat the clay-bell, and broke it – crying out the while for great wealth.

Then, out of the ground before him, rose up the figure of a white-robed woman, with long loose-flowing hair, holding a covered jar. And the woman said: 'I have come to answer your fervent prayer as it deserves to be answered. Take, therefore, this jar.' So saying, she put the jar into his hands, and disappeared.

1 A monetary unit.

Into his house the happy man rushed, to tell his wife the good news. He set down in front of her the covered jar – which was heavy – and they opened it together. And they found that it was filled, up to the very brim, with . . .

But no! – I really cannot tell you with what it was filled.

JIKININKI

Jikininki

Once, when Muso Kokushi, a priest of the Zen sect, was journeying alone through the province of Mino,[1] he lost his way in a mountain-district where there was nobody to direct him. For a long time he wandered about helplessly; and he was beginning to despair of finding shelter for the night, when he perceived, on the top of a hill lighted by the last rays of the sun, one of those little hermitages, called *anjitsu*, which are built for solitary priests. It seemed to be in ruinous condition; but he hastened to it eagerly, and found that it was inhabited by an aged priest, from whom he begged the favour of a night's lodging. This the old man harshly refused; but he directed Muso to a certain hamlet in the valley adjoining, where lodging and food could be obtained.

Muso found his way to the hamlet, which consisted of less than a dozen farm-cottages; and he was kindly received at the dwelling of the headman. Forty or fifty persons were assembled in the principal apartment, at the moment of Muso's arrival; but he was shown into a small separate room, where he was promptly supplied with food and bedding. Being very tired, he lay down to rest at an early hour; but a little before midnight he was roused from sleep by a sound of loud weeping in the next apartment. Presently the sliding-screens were gently pushed apart; and a young man, carrying a lighted lantern, entered the room, respectfully saluted him, and said: 'Reverend Sir, it is my painful duty to tell you that I am now the responsible head of this house. Yesterday I was only the eldest son. But when you came here, tired as you were, we did not wish that you should feel embarrassed in any way: therefore we did not tell you that father had died only a few hours before. The people whom you saw in the next room are the inhabitants of this village: they all assembled here to pay their last respects to the dead; and now they are going to another village, about three miles off – for by our custom, no one of us may remain in this village during the night after a death has taken place.

1 The southern part of present-day Gifu Prefecture.

We make the proper offerings and prayers – then we go away, leaving the corpse alone. Strange things always happen in the house where a corpse has thus been left: so we think that it will be better for you to come away with us. We can find you good lodging in the other village. But perhaps, as you are a priest, you have no fear of demons or evil spirits; and, if you are not afraid of being left alone with the body, you will be very welcome to the use of this poor house. However, I must tell you that nobody, except a priest, would dare to remain here tonight.'

Muso made answer: 'For your kind intention and your generous hospitality I am deeply grateful. But I am sorry that you did not tell me of your father's death when I came – for, though I was a little tired, I certainly was not so tired that I should have found difficulty in doing my duty as a priest. Had you told me, I could have performed the service before your departure. As it is, I shall perform the service after you have gone away; and I shall stay by the body until morning. I do not know what you mean by your words about the danger of staying here alone; but I am not afraid of ghosts or demons: therefore please to feel no anxiety on my account.'

The young man appeared to be rejoiced by these assurances, and expressed his gratitude in fitting words. Then the other members of the family, and the folk assembled in the adjoining room, having been told of the priest's kind promises, came to thank him – after which the master of the house said: 'Now, reverend Sir, much as we regret to leave you alone, we must bid you farewell. By the rule of our village, none of us can stay here after midnight. We beg, kind Sir, that you will take every care of your honourable body, while we are unable to attend upon you. And if you happen to hear or see anything strange during our absence, please tell us of the matter when we return in the morning.'

All then left the house, except the priest, who went to the room where the dead body was lying. The usual offerings had been set before the corpse; and a small Buddhist lamp – *tomyo* – was burning. The priest recited the service, and performed the funeral ceremonies – after which he entered into meditation. So meditating he remained through several silent hours; and there was no sound in the deserted village. But, when the hush of the night was at its deepest, there noiselessly entered a Shape, vague and vast; and in the same moment Muso found himself without power to move or speak. He saw that Shape lift the corpse, as with hands, devour it, more quickly than a cat devours a rat – beginning at the head, and eating everything: the hair and the bones and even the shroud. And the monstrous Thing, having thus consumed the body, turned to the offerings, and ate them also. Then it went away, as mysteriously as it had come.

When the villagers returned next morning, they found the priest awaiting them at the door of the headman's dwelling. All in turn saluted him; and when they had entered, and looked about the room, no-one expressed any surprise at the disappearance of the dead body and the offerings. But the master of the house said to Muso: 'Reverend Sir, you have probably seen unpleasant things during the night: all of us were anxious about you. But now we are very happy to find you alive and unharmed. Gladly we would have stayed with you, if it had been possible. But the law of our village, as I told you last evening, obliges us to quit our houses after a death has taken place, and to leave the corpse alone. Whenever this law has been broken, heretofore, some great misfortune has followed. Whenever it is obeyed, we find that the corpse and the offerings disappear during our absence. Perhaps you have seen the cause.'

Then Muso told of the dim and awful Shape that had entered the death-chamber to devour the body and the offerings. No person seemed to be surprised by his narration; and the master of the house observed: 'What you have told us, reverend Sir, agrees with what has been said about this matter from ancient time.'

Muso then inquired: 'Does not the priest on the hill sometimes perform the funeral service for your dead?'

'What priest?' the young man asked.

'The priest who yesterday evening directed me to this village,' answered Muso. 'I called at his *anjitsu* on the hill yonder. He refused me lodging, but told me the way here.'

The listeners looked at each other, as in astonishment; and, after a moment of silence, the master of the house said: 'Reverend Sir, there is no priest and there is no *anjitsu* on the hill. For the time of many generations there has not been any resident-priest in this neighbourhood.'

Muso said nothing more on the subject; for it was evident that his kind hosts supposed him to have been deluded by some goblin. But after having bidden them farewell, and obtained all necessary information as to his road, he determined to look again for the hermitage on the hill, and so to ascertain whether he had really been deceived. He found the *anjitsu* without any difficulty; and this time its aged occupant invited him to enter. When he had done so, the hermit humbly bowed down before him, exclaiming:– 'Ah! I am ashamed ! – I am very much ashamed! – I am exceedingly ashamed!'

'You need not be ashamed for having refused me shelter,' said Muso. 'You directed me to the village yonder, where I was very kindly treated; and I thank you for that favour.

'I can give no man shelter,' the recluse made answer – and it is not for the refusal that I am ashamed. I am ashamed only that you should have seen me in my real shape – for it was I who devoured the corpse and the offerings last night before your eyes . . . Know, reverend Sir, that I am a *jikininki*,[1] – an eater of human flesh. Have pity upon me, and suffer me to confess the secret fault by which I became reduced to this condition.

'A long, long time ago, I was a priest in this desolate region. There was no other priest for many leagues around. So, in that time, the bodies of the mountain-folk who died used to be brought here – sometimes from great distances – in order that I might repeat over them the holy service. But I repeated the service and performed the rites only as a matter of business – I thought only of the food and the clothes that my sacred profession enabled me to gain. And because of this selfish impiety I was reborn, immediately after my death, into the state of a *jikininki*. Since then I have been obliged to feed upon the corpses of the people who die in this district: every one of them I must devour in the way that you saw last night . . . Now, reverend Sir, let me beseech you to perform a *Segaki*-service[2] for me: help me by your prayers, I entreat you, so that I may be soon able to escape from this horrible state of existence . . . '

No sooner had the hermit uttered this petition than he disappeared; and the hermitage also disappeared at the same instant. And Muso Kokushi found himself kneeling alone in the high grass, beside an ancient and moss-grown tomb of the form called *go-rin-ishi*,[3] which seemed to be the tomb of a priest.

1 Literally, a man-eating goblin. The Japanese narrator gives also the Sanscrit term, 'Rakshasa'; but this word is quite as vague as *jikininki*, since there are many kinds of Rakshasas. Apparently the word *jikininki* signifies here one of the *Baramon-Rasetsu-Gaki* – forming the twenty-sixth class of pretas enumerated in the old Buddhist books.

2 A *Segaki*-service is a special Buddhist service performed on behalf of beings supposed to have entered into the condition of *gaki* (pretas), or hungry spirits. For a brief account of such a service, see my *Japanese Miscellany*.

3 Literally, 'five-circle or five-zone stone'. A funeral monument consisting of five parts superimposed – each of a different form – symbolizing the five mystic elements: Ether, Air, Fire, Water, Earth.

MUJINA

Mujina

On the Akasaka Road, in Tokyo, there is a slope called Kii-no-kuni-zaka – which means the Slope of the Province of Kii. I do not know why it is called the Slope of the Province of Kii. On one side of this slope you see an ancient moat, deep and very wide, with high green banks rising up to some place of gardens – and on the other side of the road extend the long and lofty walls of an imperial palace. Before the era of street-lamps and jinrikishas, this neighbourhood was very lonesome after dark; and belated pedestrians would go miles out of their way rather than mount the Kii-no-kuni-zaka, alone, after sunset.

All because of a Mujina that used to walk there.[1]

The last man who saw the Mujina was an old merchant of the Kyobashi quarter, who died about thirty years ago. This is the story, as he told it. One night, at a late hour, he was hurrying up the Kii-no-kuni-zaka, when he perceived a woman crouching by the moat, all alone, and weeping bitterly. Fearing that she intended to drown herself, he stopped to offer her any assistance or consolation in his power. She appeared to be a slight and graceful person, handsomely dressed; and her hair was arranged like that of a young girl of good family. 'O-jochu',[2] he exclaimed, approaching her – 'O-jochu, do not cry like that! . . . Tell me what the trouble is; and if there be any way to help you, I shall be glad to help you.' (He really meant what he said; for he was a very kind man.) But she continued to weep – hiding her face from him with one of her long sleeves. 'O-jochu,' he said again, as gently as he could – 'please, please listen to me! . . . This is no place for a young lady at night! Do not cry, I implore you! – only tell me how I may be of some help to you!' Slowly she rose up, but turned her back to him, and continued to moan and sob behind her

1 A kind of badger. Certain animals were thought to be able to transform themselves and cause mischief for humans.
2 O-jochu ('honorable damsel'), a polite form of address used in speaking to a young lady whom one does not know.

sleeve. He laid his hand lightly upon her shoulder, and pleaded:– 'O-jochu! – O-jochu! – O-jochu! . . . Listen to me, just for one little moment! . . . O-jochu! – O-jochu!' . . . Then that O-jochu turned around, and dropped her sleeve, and stroked her face with her hand – and the man saw that she had no eyes or nose or mouth – and he screamed and ran away.[1]

Up Kii-no-kuni-zaka he ran and ran; and all was black and empty before him. On and on he ran, never daring to look back; and at last he saw a lantern, so far away that it looked like the gleam of a firefly; and he made for it. It proved to be only the lantern of an itinerant *soba*-seller,[2] who had set down his stand by the road-side; but any light and any human companionship was good after that experience; and he flung himself down at the feet of the *soba*-seller, crying out, 'Ah! – aa!! – *aa!!!*' . . .

'*Kore! kore!*'[3] roughly exclaimed the *soba*-man. 'Here! What is the matter with you? Anybody hurt you?'

'No – nobody hurt me,' panted the other – 'only . . . *Ah! – aa!*'

' – Only scared you?' queried the peddler, unsympathetically. 'Robbers?'

'Not robbers – not robbers,' gasped the terrified man . . . 'I saw . . . I saw a woman – by the moat – and she showed me . . . *Aa!* I cannot tell you what she showed me! . . . '

'*He!*[4] Was it anything like THIS that she showed you?' cried the *soba*-man, stroking his own face – which therewith became like unto an Egg . . . And, simultaneously, the light went out.

1 An apparition with a smooth, totally featureless face, called a *nopperabo*, is a stock part of the Japanese pantheon of ghosts and demons.
2 *Soba* is a preparation of buckwheat, somewhat resembling vermicelli.
3 An exclamation of annoyed alarm.
4 Well!

ROKURO-KUBI

Rokuro-Kubi

Nearly five hundred years ago there was a samurai, named Isogai Heidazaemon Taketsura, in the service of the Lord Kikuji, of Kyushu. This Isogai had inherited, from many warlike ancestors, a natural aptitude for military exercises, and extraordinary strength. While yet a boy he had surpassed his teachers in the art of swordsmanship, in archery, and in the use of the spear, and had displayed all the capacities of a daring and skilful soldier. Afterwards, in the time of the Eikyo[1] war, he so distinguished himself that high honours were bestowed upon him. But when the house of Kikuji came to ruin, Isogai found himself without a master. He might then easily have obtained service under another daimyo; but as he had never sought distinction for his own sake alone, and as his heart remained true to his former lord, he preferred to give up the world. So he cut off his hair, and became a travelling priest – taking the Buddhist name of Kwairyo.

But always, under the *koromo*[2] of the priest, Kwairyo kept warm within him the heart of the samurai. As in other years he had laughed at peril, so now also he scorned danger; and in all weathers and all seasons he journeyed to preach the good Law in places where no other priest would have dared to go. For that age was an age of violence and disorder; and upon the highways there was no security for the solitary traveller, even if he happened to be a priest.

In the course of his first long journey, Kwairyo had occasion to visit the province of Kai.[3] One evening, as he was travelling through the mountains of that province, darkness overcame him in a very lonesome district, leagues away from any village. So he resigned himself to pass the night under the stars; and having found a suitable grassy spot, by the roadside, he lay down there, and prepared to sleep. He had always welcomed discomfort; and even a bare rock was for him a

---

1 The period of Eikyo lasted from 1429 to 1441.
2 The upper robe of a Buddhist priest is thus called.
3 Present-day Yamanashi Prefecture.

good bed, when nothing better could be found, and the root of a pine tree an excellent pillow. His body was iron; and he never troubled himself about dews or rain or frost or snow.

Scarcely had he lain down when a man came along the road, carrying an axe and a great bundle of chopped wood. This woodcutter halted on seeing Kwairyo lying down, and, after a moment of silent observation, said to him in a tone of great surprise: 'What kind of a man can you be, good Sir, that you dare to lie down alone in such a place as this? . . . There are haunters about here – many of them. are you not afraid of Hairy Things?'

'My friend,' cheerfully answered Kwairyo, 'I am only a wandering priest – a "Cloud-and-Water-Guest", as folks call it: *Unsui-no-ryokaku*.[1] And I am not in the least afraid of Hairy Things – if you mean goblin-foxes, or goblin-badgers, or any creatures of that kind. As for lonesome places, I like them: they are suitable for meditation. I am accustomed to sleeping in the open air; and I have learned never to be anxious about my life.'

'You must be indeed a brave man, Sir Priest,' the peasant responded, 'to lie down here! This place has a bad name – a very bad name. But, as the proverb has it, *Kunshi ayayuki ni chikayorazu* [the superior man does not needlessly expose himself to peril]; and I must assure you, Sir, that it is very dangerous to sleep here. Therefore, although my house is only a wretched thatched hut, let me beg of you to come home with me at once. In the way of food, I have nothing to offer you; but there is a roof at least, and you can sleep under it without risk.'

He spoke earnestly; and Kwairyo, liking the kindly tone of the man, accepted this modest offer. The woodcutter guided him along a narrow path, leading up from the main road through mountain-forest. It was a rough and dangerous path – sometimes skirting precipices – sometimes offering nothing but a network of slippery roots for the foot to rest upon – sometimes winding over or between masses of jagged rock. But at last Kwairyo found himself upon a cleared space at the top of a hill, with a full moon shining overhead; and he saw before him a small thatched cottage, cheerfully lighted from within. The woodcutter led him to a shed at the back of the house, whither water had been conducted, through bamboo-pipes, from some neighbouring stream; and the two men washed their feet. Beyond the shed was a vegetable garden, and a grove of cedars and bamboos; and beyond the trees appeared the glimmer of a cascade,

1 A term for itinerant priests.

pouring from some loftier height, and swaying in the moonshine like a long white robe.

As Kwairyo entered the cottage with his guide, he perceived four persons – men and women – warming their hands at a little fire kindled in the *ro*[1] of the principle apartment. They bowed low to the priest, and greeted him in the most respectful manner. Kwairyo wondered that persons so poor, and dwelling in such a solitude, should be aware of the polite forms of greeting. 'These are good people,' he thought to himself; 'and they must have been taught by someone well acquainted with the rules of propriety.' Then turning to his host – the *aruji*, or house-master, as the others called him – Kwairyo said: 'From the kindness of your speech, and from the very polite welcome given me by your household, I imagine that you have not always been a woodcutter. Perhaps you formerly belonged to one of the upper classes?'

Smiling, the woodcutter answered: 'Sir, you are not mistaken. Though now living as you find me, I was once a person of some distinction. My story is the story of a ruined life – ruined by my own fault. I used to be in the service of a daimyo; and my rank in that service was not inconsiderable. But I loved women and wine too well; and under the influence of passion I acted wickedly. My selfishness brought about the ruin of our house, and caused the death of many persons. Retribution followed me; and I long remained a fugitive in the land. Now I often pray that I may be able to make some atonement for the evil which I did, and to re-establish the ancestral home. But I fear that I shall never find any way of so doing. Nevertheless, I try to overcome the karma of my errors by sincere repentance, and by helping as far as I can, those who are unfortunate.'

Kwairyo was pleased by this announcement of good resolve; and he said to the *aruji*: 'My friend, I have had occasion to observe that men prone to folly in their youth, may in after years become very earnest in right living. In the holy sutras it is written that those strongest in wrong-doing can become, by power of good resolve, the strongest in right-doing. I do not doubt that you have a good heart; and I hope that better fortune will come to you. Tonight I shall recite the sutras for your sake, and pray that you may obtain the force to overcome the karma of any past errors.'

1 A sort of little fireplace, contrived in the floor of a room, is thus described. The *ro* is usually a square shallow cavity, lined with metal and half-filled with ashes, in which charcoal is lighted.

With these assurances, Kwairyo bade the *aruji* good-night; and his host showed him to a very small side-room, where a bed had been made ready. Then all went to sleep except the priest, who began to read the sutras by the light of a paper lantern. Until a late hour he continued to read and pray: then he opened a little window in his little sleeping-room, to take a last look at the landscape before lying down. The night was beautiful: there was no cloud in the sky: there was no wind; and the strong moonlight threw down sharp black shadows of foliage, and glittered on the dews of the garden. Shrillings of crickets and bell-insects[1] made a musical tumult; and the sound of the neighbouring cascade deepened with the night. Kwairyo felt thirsty as he listened to the noise of the water; and, remembering the bamboo aqueduct at the rear of the house, he thought that he could go there and get a drink without disturbing the sleeping household. Very gently he pushed apart the sliding-screens that separated his room from the main apartment; and he saw, by the light of the lantern, five recumbent bodies – without heads!

For one instant he stood bewildered – imagining a crime. But in another moment he perceived that there was no blood, and that the headless necks did not look as if they had been cut. Then he thought to himself: 'Either this is an illusion made by goblins, or I have been lured into the dwelling of a Rokuro-Kubi[2]... In the book *Soshinki*[3] it is written that if one find the body of a Rokuro-Kubi without its head, and remove the body to another place, the head will never be able to join itself again to the neck. And the book further says that when the head comes back and finds that its body has been moved, it will strike itself upon the floor three times – bounding like a ball – and will pant as in great fear, and presently die. Now, if these be Rokuro-Kubi, they mean me no good – so I shall be justified in following the instructions of the book . . . '

He seized the body of the *aruji* by the feet, pulled it to the window, and pushed it out. Then he went to the back door, which he found barred; and he surmised that the heads had made their exit through the smoke-hole in the roof, which had been left open. Gently un-barring the door, he made his way to the garden, and proceeded with all possible caution to the grove beyond it. He heard voices talking in the grove; and he went in the direction of the voices – stealing from

1 Direct translation of '*suzumushi*', a kind of cricket with a distinctive chirp like a tiny bell, whence the name.
2 Now a Rokuro-Kubi is ordinarily conceived as a goblin whose neck stretches out to great lengths, but which nevertheless always remains attached to its body.
3 A Chinese collection of stories on the supernatural.

shadow to shadow, until he reached a good hiding-place. Then, from behind a trunk, he caught sight of the heads – all five of them – flitting about, and chatting as they flitted. They were eating worms and insects which they found on the ground or among the trees. Presently the head of the *aruji* stopped eating and said: 'Ah, that travelling priest who came tonight – how fat all his body is! When we shall have eaten him, our bellies will be well filled . . . I was foolish to talk to him as I did – it only set him to reciting the sutras on behalf of my soul! To go near him while he is reciting would be difficult; and we cannot touch him so long as he is praying. But as it is now nearly morning, perhaps he has gone to sleep . . . Some one of you go to the house and see what the fellow is doing.'

Another head – the head of a young woman – immediately rose up and flitted to the house, lightly as a bat. After a few minutes it came back, and cried out huskily, in a tone of great alarm: 'That travelling priest is not in the house – he is gone! But that is not the worst of the matter. He has taken the body of our *aruji*; and I do not know where he has put it.'

At this announcement the head of the *aruji* – distinctly visible in the moonlight – assumed a frightful aspect: its eyes opened monstrously; its hair stood up bristling; and its teeth gnashed. Then a cry burst from its lips; and – weeping tears of rage – it exclaimed: 'Since my body has been moved, to rejoin it is not possible! Then I must die! . . . And all through the work of that priest! Before I die I will get at that priest! – I will tear him! – I will devour him! . . . *and there he is* – behind that tree! – hiding behind that tree! See him – the fat coward! . . . '

In the same moment the head of the *aruji*, followed by the other four heads, sprang at Kwairyo. But the strong priest had already armed himself by plucking up a young tree; and with that tree he struck the heads as they came – knocking them from him with tremendous blows. Four of them fled away. But the head of the *aruji*, though battered again and again, desperately continued to bound at the priest, and at last caught him by the left sleeve of his robe. Kwairyo, however, as quickly gripped the head by its topknot, and repeatedly struck it. It did not release its hold; but it uttered a long moan, and thereafter ceased to struggle. It was dead. But its teeth still held the sleeve; and, for all his great strength, Kwairyo could not force open the jaws.

With the head still hanging to his sleeve he went back to the house, and there caught sight of the other four Rokuro-Kubi squatting together, with their bruised and bleeding heads reunited to their bodies. But when they perceived him at the back door all screamed, 'The priest! the priest!' – and fled, through the other doorway, out into the woods.

Eastward the sky was brightening; day was about to dawn; and Kwairyo knew that the power of the goblins was limited to the hours of darkness. He looked at the head clinging to his sleeve – its face all fouled with blood and foam and clay; and he laughed aloud as he thought to himself: '*What a miyage*![1] – the head of a goblin!' After which he gathered together his few belongings, and leisurely descended the mountain to continue his journey.

Right on he journeyed, until he came to Suwa in Shinano;[2] and into the main street of Suwa he solemnly strode, with the head dangling at his elbow. Then woman fainted, and children screamed and ran away; and there was a great crowding and clamouring until the *torite* (as the police in those days were called) seized the priest, and took him to jail. For they supposed the head to be the head of a murdered man who, in the moment of being killed, had caught the murderer's sleeve in his teeth. As for Kwairyo, he only smiled and said nothing when they questioned him. So, after having passed a night in prison, he was brought before the magistrates of the district. Then he was ordered to explain how he, a priest, had been found with the head of a man fastened to his sleeve, and why he had dared thus shamelessly to parade his crime in the sight of people.

Kwairyo laughed long and loudly at these questions; and then he said: 'Sirs, I did not fasten the head to my sleeve: it fastened itself there – much against my will. And I have not committed any crime. For this is not the head of a man; it is the head of a goblin – and, if I caused the death of the goblin, I did not do so by any shedding of blood, but simply by taking the precautions necessary to assure my own safety . . . ' And he proceeded to relate the whole of the adventure – bursting into another hearty laugh as he told of his encounter with the five heads.

But the magistrates did not laugh. They judged him to be a hardened criminal, and his story an insult to their intelligence. Therefore, without further questioning, they decided to order his immediate execution – all of them except one, a very old man. This

---

1 A present made to friends or to the household on returning from a journey is thus called. Ordinarily, of course, the *miyage* consists of something produced in the locality to which the journey has been made: this is the point of Kwairyo's jest.
2 Present-day Nagano Prefecture.

aged officer had made no remark during the trial; but, after having heard the opinion of his colleagues, he rose up, and said: 'Let us first examine the head carefully; for this, I think, has not yet been done. If the priest has spoken truth, the head itself should bear witness for him . . . Bring the head here!'

So the head, still holding in its teeth the *koromo* that had been stripped from Kwairyo's shoulders, was put before the judges. The old man turned it round and round, carefully examined it, and discovered, on the nape of its neck, several strange red characters. He called the attention of his colleagues to these, and also bade them observe that the edges of the neck nowhere presented the appearance of having been cut by any weapon. On the contrary, the line of severance was smooth as the line at which a falling leaf detaches itself from the stem . . . Then said the elder: 'I am quite sure that the priest told us nothing but the truth. This is the head of a Rokuro-Kubi. In the book *Nan-ho-I-butsu-shi* it is written that certain red characters can always be found upon the nape of the neck of a real Rokuro-Kubi. There are the characters: you can see for yourselves that they have not been painted. Moreover, it is well known that such goblins have been dwelling in the mountains of the province of Kai from very ancient time . . . But you, Sir,' he exclaimed, turning to Kwairyo – 'what sort of sturdy priest may you be? Certainly you have given proof of a courage that few priests possess; and you have the air of a soldier rather than a priest. Perhaps you once belonged to the samurai-class?'

'You have guessed rightly, Sir,' Kwairyo responded. 'Before becoming a priest, I long followed the profession of arms; and in those days I never feared man or devil. My name then was Isogai Heidazaemon Taketsura of Kyushu: there may be some among you who remember it.'

At the mention of that name, a murmur of admiration filled the court-room.; for there were many present who remembered it. And Kwairyo immediately found himself among friends instead of judges – friends anxious to prove their admiration by fraternal kindness. With honour they escorted him to the residence of the daimyo, who welcomed him, and feasted him, and made him a handsome present before allowing him to depart. When Kwairyo left Suwa, he was as happy as any priest is permitted to be in this transitory world. As for the head, he took it with him – jocosely insisting that he intended it for a *miyage*.

And now it only remains to tell what became of the head.

A day or two after leaving Suwa, Kwairyo met with a robber, who stopped him in a lonesome place, and bade him strip. Kwairyo at once removed his *koromo*, and offered it to the robber, who then first perceived what was hanging to the sleeve. Though brave, the highwayman was startled: he dropped the garment, and sprang back. Then he cried out:– 'You! – what kind of a priest are you? Why, you are a worse man than I am! It is true that I have killed people; but I never walked about with anybody's head fastened to my sleeve . . . Well, Sir priest, I suppose we are of the same calling; and I must say that I admire you! . . . Now that head would be of use to me: I could frighten people with it. Will you sell it? You can have my robe in exchange for your *koromo*; and I will give you five *ryo* for the head.'

Kwairyo answered: 'I shall let you have the head and the robe if you insist; but I must tell you that this is not the head of a man. It is a goblin's head. So, if you buy it, and have any trouble in consequence, please to remember that you were not deceived by me.'

'What a nice priest you are!' exclaimed the robber. 'You kill men, and jest about it! . . . But I am really in earnest. Here is my robe; and here is the money – and let me have the head . . . What is the use of joking?'

'Take the thing,' said Kwairyo. 'I was not joking. The only joke – if there be any joke at all – is that you are fool enough to pay good money for a goblin's head.' And Kwairyo, loudly laughing, went upon his way.

Thus the robber got the head and the *koromo*; and for some time he played goblin-priest upon the highways. But, reaching the neighbourhood of Suwa, he there learned the true story of the head; and he then became afraid that the spirit of the Rokuro-Kubi might give him trouble. So he made up his mind to take back the head to the place from which it had come, and to bury it with its body. He found his way to the lonely cottage in the mountains of Kai; but nobody was there, and he could not discover the body. Therefore he buried the head by itself, in the grove behind the cottage; and he had a tombstone set up over the grave; and he caused a *Segaki*-service to be performed on behalf of the spirit of the Rokuro-Kubi. And that tombstone – known as the Tombstone of the Rokuro-Kubi – may be seen (at least so the Japanese story-teller declares) even unto this day.

A DEAD SECRET

A Dead Secret

A long time ago, in the province of Tamba,[1] there lived a rich merchant named Inamuraya Gensuke. He had a daughter called O-Sono. As she was very clever and pretty, he thought it would be a pity to let her grow up with only such teaching as the country teachers could give her: so he sent her, in care of some trusty attendants, to Kyoto, that she might be trained in the polite accomplishments taught to the ladies of the capital. After she had thus been educated, she was married to a friend of her father's family – a merchant named Nagaraya – and she lived happily with him for nearly four years. They had one child – but O-Sono fell ill and died, in the fourth year after her marriage.

On the night after the funeral of O-Sono, her little son said that his mamma had come back, and was in the room upstairs. She had smiled at him, but would not talk to him: so he became afraid, and ran away. Then some of the family went upstairs to the room which had been O-Sono's; and they were startled to see, by the light of a small lamp which had been kindled before a shrine in that room, the figure of the dead mother. She appeared as if standing in front of a *tansu*, or chest of drawers, that still contained her ornaments and her wearing-apparel. Her head and shoulders could be very distinctly seen; but from the waist downwards the figure thinned into invisibility – it was like an imperfect reflection of her, and transparent as a shadow on water.

Then the folk were afraid, and left the room. Below they consulted together; and the mother of O-Sono's husband said: 'A woman is fond of her small things; and O-Sono was much attached to her belongings. Perhaps she has come back to look at them. Many dead persons will do that – unless the things be given to the parish-temple. If we present O-Sono's robes and girdles to the temple, her spirit will probably find rest.'

1 On the present-day map, Tamba corresponds roughly to the central area of Kyoto Prefecture and part of Hyogo Prefecture.

It was agreed that this should be done as soon as possible. So on the following morning the drawers were emptied; and all of O-Sono's ornaments and dresses were taken to the temple. But she came back the next night, and looked at the *tansu* as before. And she came back also on the night following, and the night after that, and every night – and the house became a house of fear.

The mother of O-Sono's husband then went to the parish-temple, and told the chief priest all that had happened, and asked for ghostly counsel. The temple was a Zen temple; and the head-priest was a learned old man, known as Daigen Osho. He said: 'There must be something about which she is anxious, in or near that *tansu*.' – 'But we emptied all the drawers,' replied the woman – 'there is nothing in the *tansu*.' – 'Well,' said Daigen Osho, 'tonight I shall go to your house, and keep watch in that room, and see what can be done. You must give orders that no person shall enter the room while I am watching, unless I call.'

After sundown, Daigen Osho went to the house, and found the room made ready for him. He remained there alone, reading the sutras; and nothing appeared until after the Hour of the Rat.[1] Then the figure of O-Sono suddenly outlined itself in front of the *tansu*. Her face had a wistful look; and she kept her eyes fixed upon the *tansu*.

The priest uttered the holy formula prescribed in such cases, and then, addressing the figure by the *kaimyo*[2] of O-Sono, said: 'I have come here in order to help you. Perhaps in that *tansu* there is something about which you have reason to feel anxious. Shall I try to find it for you?' The shadow appeared to give assent by a slight motion of the head; and the priest, rising, opened the top drawer. It was empty. Successively he opened the second, the third, and the fourth drawer – he searched carefully behind them and beneath them – he carefully examined the interior of the chest. He found nothing. But the figure remained gazing as wistfully as before. 'What can she want?' thought the priest. Suddenly it occurred to him that there might be something hidden under the paper with

1 The Hour of the Rat (*Ne-no-Koku*), according to the old Japanese method of reckoning time, was the first hour. It corresponded to the time between our midnight and two o'clock in the morning; for the ancient Japanese hours were each equal to two modern hours.

2 *Kaimyo*, the posthumous Buddhist name, or religious name, given to the dead. Strictly speaking, the meaning of the work is sila-name. (See my paper entitled, 'The Literature of the Dead' in *Exotics and Retrospectives*.)

which the drawers were lined. He removed the lining of the first drawer – nothing! He removed the lining of the second and third drawers – still nothing. But under the lining of the lowermost drawer he found – a letter. 'Is this the thing about which you have been troubled?' he asked. The shadow of the woman turned toward him – her faint gaze fixed upon the letter. 'Shall I burn it for you?' he asked. She bowed before him. 'It shall be burned in the temple this very morning,' he promised – 'and no-one shall read it, except myself.' The figure smiled and vanished.

Dawn was breaking as the priest descended the stairs, to find the family waiting anxiously below. 'Do not be anxious,' he said to them. 'She will not appear again.' And she never did.

The letter was burned. It was a love-letter written to O-Sono in the time of her studies at Kyoto. But the priest alone knew what was in it; and the secret died with him.

YUKI-ONNA

Yuki-Onna

In a village of Musashi Province,[1] there lived two woodcutters: Mosaku and Minokichi. At the time of which I am speaking, Mosaku was an old man; and Minokichi, his apprentice, was a lad of eighteen years. Every day they went together to a forest situated about five miles from their village. On the way to that forest there is a wide river to cross; and there is a ferry-boat. Several times a bridge was built where the ferry is; but the bridge was each time carried away by a flood. No common bridge can resist the current there when the river rises.

Mosaku and Minokichi were on their way home, one very cold evening, when a great snowstorm overtook them. They reached the ferry; and they found that the boatman had gone away, leaving his boat on the other side of the river. It was no day for swimming; and the woodcutters took shelter in the ferryman's hut – thinking themselves lucky to find any shelter at all. There was no brazier in the hut, nor any place in which to make a fire: it was only a two-mat[2] hut, with a single door, but no window. Mosaku and Minokichi fastened the door, and lay down to rest, with their straw rain-coats over them. At first they did not feel very cold; and they thought that the storm would soon be over.

The old man almost immediately fell asleep; but the boy, Minokichi, lay awake a long time, listening to the awful wind, and the continual slashing of the snow against the door. The river was roaring; and the hut swayed and creaked like a junk at sea. It was a terrible storm; and the air was every moment becoming colder; and Minokichi shivered under his rain-coat. But at last, in spite of the cold, he too fell asleep.

He was awakened by a showering of snow in his face. The door of the hut had been forced open; and, by the snow-light (*yuki-akari*), he

1 An ancient province whose boundaries took in most of present-day Tokyo, and parts of Saitama and Kanagawa prefectures.
2 That is to say, with a floor-surface of about six feet square.

saw a woman in the room – a woman all in white. She was bending above Mosaku, and blowing her breath upon him – and her breath was like a bright white smoke. Almost in the same moment she turned to Minokichi, and stooped over him. He tried to cry out, but found that he could not utter any sound. The white woman bent down over him, lower and lower, until her face almost touched him; and he saw that she was very beautiful – though her eyes made him afraid. For a little time she continued to look at him – then she smiled, and she whispered: 'I intended to treat you like the other man. But I cannot help feeling some pity for you – because you are so young . . . You are a pretty boy, Minokichi; and I will not hurt you now. But, if you ever tell anybody – even your own mother – about what you have seen this night, I shall know it; and then I will kill you . . . Remember what I say!'

With these words, she turned from him, and passed through the doorway. Then he found himself able to move; and he sprang up, and looked out. But the woman was nowhere to be seen; and the snow was driving furiously into the hut. Minokichi closed the door, and secured it by fixing several billets of wood against it. He wondered if the wind had blown it open – he thought that he might have been only dreaming, and might have mistaken the gleam of the snow-light in the doorway for the figure of a white woman: but he could not be sure. He called to Mosaku, and was frightened because the old man did not answer. He put out his hand in the dark, and touched Mosaku's face, and found that it was ice! Mosaku was stark and dead . . .

By dawn the storm was over; and when the ferryman returned to his station, a little after sunrise, he found Minokichi lying senseless beside the frozen body of Mosaku. Minokichi was promptly cared for, and soon came to himself; but he remained a long time ill from the effects of the cold of that terrible night. He had been greatly frightened also by the old man's death; but he said nothing about the vision of the woman in white. As soon as he got well again, he returned to his calling – going alone every morning to the forest, and coming back at nightfall with his bundles of wood, which his mother helped him to sell.

One evening, in the winter of the following year, as he was on his way home, he overtook a girl who happened to be travelling by the same road. She was a tall, slim girl, very good-looking; and she answered Minokichi's greeting in a voice as pleasant to the ear as the voice of a song-bird. Then he walked beside her; and they began to talk. The girl said that her name was O-Yuki;[1] that she had lately lost both of her parents; and that she was going to Yedo,[2] where she happened to have some poor relations, who might help her to find a situation as a servant. Minokichi soon felt charmed by this strange girl; and the more that he looked at her, the handsomer she appeared to be. He asked her whether she was yet betrothed; and she answered, laughingly, that she was free. Then, in her turn, she asked Minokichi whether he was married, or pledged to marry; and he told her that, although he had only a widowed mother to support, the question of an 'honourable daughter-in-law' had not yet been considered, as he was very young . . . After these confidences, they walked on for a long while without speaking; but, as the proverb declares, *Ki ga areba, me mo kuchi hodo ni mono wo iu*: 'When the wish is there, the eyes can say as much as the mouth.' By the time they reached the village, they had become very much pleased with each other; and then Minokichi asked O-Yuki to rest awhile at his house. After some shy hesitation, she went there with him; and his mother made her welcome, and prepared a warm meal for her. O-Yuki behaved so nicely that Minokichi's mother took a sudden fancy to her, and persuaded her to delay her journey to Yedo. And the natural end of the matter was that Yuki never went to Yedo at all. She remained in the house, as an 'honourable daughter-in-law'.

O-Yuki proved a very good daughter-in-law. When Minokichi's mother came to die – some five years later – her last words were words of affection and praise for the wife of her son. And O-Yuki bore Minokichi ten children, boys and girls – handsome children all of them, and very fair of skin.

The country-folk thought O-Yuki a wonderful person, by nature different from themselves. Most of the peasant-women age early; but O-Yuki, even after having become the mother of ten children, looked as young and fresh as on the day when she had first come to the village.

One night, after the children had gone to sleep, O-Yuki was sewing by the light of a paper lamp; and Minokichi, watching her, said: 'To

1 This name, signifying 'Snow', is not uncommon. On the subject of Japanese female names, see my paper in the volume entitled *Shadowings*.
2 Also spelled Edo, the former name of Tokyo.

see you sewing there, with the light on your face, makes me think of a strange thing that happened when I was a lad of eighteen. I then saw somebody as beautiful and white as you are now – indeed, she was very like you . . . '

Without lifting her eyes from her work, O-Yuki responded: 'Tell me about her . . . Where did you see her?'

Then Minokichi told her about the terrible night in the ferryman's hut – and about the White Woman that had stooped above him, smiling and whispering – and about the silent death of old Mosaku. And he said: 'Asleep or awake, that was the only time that I saw a being as beautiful as you. Of course, she was not a human being; and I was afraid of her – very much afraid – but she was so white! . . . Indeed, I have never been sure whether it was a dream that I saw, or the Woman of the Snow . . . '

O-Yuki flung down her sewing, and arose, and bowed above Minokichi where he sat, and shrieked into his face: 'It was I – I – I! Yuki it was! And I told you then that I would kill you if you ever said one word about it! . . . But for those children asleep there, I would kill you this moment! And now you had better take very, very good care of them; for if ever they have reason to complain of you, I will treat you as you deserve! . . . '

Even as she screamed, her voice became thin, like a crying of wind – then she melted into a bright white mist that spired to the roof-beams, and shuddered away through the smoke-hole . . . Never again was she seen.

THE STORY OF AOYAGI

THE TALE OF ASLAN

The Story of Aoyagi

In the era of Bummei [1469-1486] there was a young samurai called Tomotada in the service of Hatakeyama Yoshimune, the Lord of Noto.[1] Tomotada was a native of Echizen;[2] but at an early age he had been taken, as page, into the palace of the daimyo of Noto, and had been educated, under the supervision of that prince, for the profession of arms. As he grew up, he proved himself both a good scholar and a good soldier, and continued to enjoy the favour of his prince. Being gifted with an amiable character, a winning address, and a very handsome person, he was admired and much liked by his samurai-comrades.

When Tomotada was about twenty years old, he was sent upon a private mission to Hosokawa Masamoto, the great daimyo of Kyoto, a kinsman of Hatakeyama Yoshimune. Having been ordered to journey through Echizen, the youth requested and obtained permission to pay a visit, on the way, to his widowed mother.

It was the coldest period of the year when he started; and, though mounted upon a powerful horse, he found himself obliged to proceed slowly. The road which he followed passed through a mountain-district where the settlements were few and far between; and on the second day of his journey, after a weary ride of hours, he was dismayed to find that he could not reached his intended halting-place until late in the night. He had reason to be anxious – for a heavy snowstorm came on, with an intensely cold wind; and the horse showed signs of exhaustion. But in that trying moment, Tomotada unexpectedly perceived the thatched room of a cottage on the summit of a near hill, where willow-trees were growing. With difficulty he urged his tired animal to the dwelling; and he loudly knocked upon the storm-doors, which had been closed against the wind. An

1 An ancient province corresponding to the northern part of present-day Ishikawa Prefecture.
2 An ancient province corresponding to the eastern part of present-day Fukui Prefecture.

old woman opened them, and cried out compassionately at the sight of the handsome stranger: 'Ah, how pitiful! – a young gentleman travelling alone in such weather! . . . Deign, young master, to enter.'

Tomotada dismounted, and after leading his horse to a shed in the rear, entered the cottage, where he saw an old man and a girl warming themselves by a fire of bamboo splints. They respectfully invited him to approach the fire; and the old folks then proceeded to warm some rice-wine, and to prepare food for the traveller, whom they ventured to question in regard to his journey. Meanwhile the young girl disappeared behind a screen. Tomotada had observed, with astonishment, that she was extremely beautiful – though her attire was of the most wretched kind, and her long, loose hair in disorder. He wondered that so handsome a girl should be living in such a miserable and lonesome place.

The old man said to him: 'Honoured Sir, the next village is far; and the snow is falling thickly. The wind is piercing; and the road is very bad. Therefore, to proceed further this night would probably be dangerous. Although this hovel is unworthy of your presence, and although we have not any comfort to offer, perhaps it were safer to remain tonight under this miserable roof . . . We would take good care of your horse.'

Tomotada accepted this humble proposal – secretly glad of the chance thus afforded him to see more of the young girl. Presently a coarse but ample meal was set before him; and the girl came from behind the screen, to serve the wine. She was now reclad, in a rough but cleanly robe of homespun; and her long, loose hair had been neatly combed and smoothed. As she bent forward to fill his cup, Tomotada was amazed to perceive that she was incomparably more beautiful than any woman whom he had ever before seen; and there was a grace about her every motion that astonished him. But the elders began to apologise for her, saying: 'Sir, our daughter, Aoyagi,[1] has been brought up here in the mountains, almost alone; and she knows nothing of gentle service. We pray that you will pardon her stupidity and her ignorance.' Tomotada protested that he deemed himself lucky to be waited upon by so comely a maiden. He could not turn his eyes away from her – though he saw that his admiring gaze made her blush – and he left the wine and food untasted before him. The mother said: 'Kind Sir, we very much hope that you will try to eat and to drink a little – though our peasant-fare is of the worst – as

1 The name signifies 'Green Willow' – though rarely met with, it is still in use.

you must have been chilled by that piercing wind.' Then, to please
the old folks, Tomotada ate and drank as he could; but the charm of
the blushing girl still grew upon him. He talked with her, and found
that her speech was sweet as her face. Brought up in the mountains
she might have been – but, in that case, her parents must at some
time been persons of high degree; for she spoke and moved like a
damsel of rank. Suddenly he addressed her with a poem – which was
also a question – inspired by the delight in his heart:

> *Tadzunetsuru,*
> *Hana ka tote koso,*
> *Hi wo kurase,*
> *Akenu ni otoru*
> *Akane sasuran?*

[Being on my way to pay a visit, I found that which I took to be
a flower: therefore here I spend the day . . . Why, in the time
before dawn, the dawn-blush tint should glow – that, indeed, I
know not.] [1]

Without a moment's hesitation, she answered him in these verses:

> *Izuru hi no*
> *Honomeku iro wo*
> *Waga sode ni*
> *Tsutsumaba asu mo*
> *Kimiya tomaran.*

[If with my sleeve I hide the faint fair colour of the dawning sun –
then, perhaps, in the morning my lord will remain.'] [2]

Then Tomotada knew that she accepted his admiration; and he
was scarcely less surprised by the art with which she had uttered her
feelings in verse, than delighted by the assurance which the verses
conveyed. He was now certain that in all this world he could not
hope to meet, much less to win, a girl more beautiful and witty than

1 The poem may be read in two ways; several of the phrases having a double
meaning. But the art of its construction would need considerable space to
explain, and could scarcely interest the Western reader. The meaning which
Tomotada desired to convey might be thus expressed: 'While journeying to visit
my mother, I met with a being lovely as a flower; and for the sake of that lovely
person, I am passing the day here . . . Fair one, wherefore that dawn-like blush
before the hour of dawn? – Can it mean that you love me?'
2 Another reading is possible; but this one gives the signification of the *answer*
intended.

this rustic maid before him; and a voice in his heart seemed to cry out
urgently, 'Take the luck that the gods have put in your way!' In short
he was bewitched – bewitched to such a degree that, without further
preliminary, he asked the old people to give him their daughter in
marriage – telling them, at the same time, his name and lineage, and
his rank in the train of the Lord of Noto.

They bowed down before him, with many exclamations of grateful
astonishment. But, after some moments of apparent hesitation, the
father replied: 'Honoured master, you are a person of high position,
and likely to rise to still higher things. Too great is the favour that
you deign to offer us – indeed, the depth of our gratitude therefor is
not to be spoken or measured. But this girl of ours, being a stupid
country-girl of vulgar birth, with no training or teaching of any sort,
it would be improper to let her become the wife of a noble samurai.
Even to speak of such a matter is not right . . . But, since you find the
girl to your liking, and have condescended to pardon her peasant-
manners and to overlook her great rudeness, we do gladly present
her to you, for an humble handmaid. Deign, therefore, to act here-
after in her regard according to your august pleasure.'

Ere morning the storm had passed; and day broke through a
cloudless east. Even if the sleeve of Aoyagi hid from her lover's eyes
the rose-blush of that dawn, he could no longer tarry. But neither
could he resign himself to part with the girl; and, when everything
had been prepared for his journey, he thus addressed her parents:
'Though it may seem thankless to ask for more than I have already
received, I must again beg you to give me your daughter for wife. It
would be difficult for me to separate from her now; and as she is
willing to accompany me, if you permit, I can take her with me as she
is. If you will give her to me, I shall ever cherish you as parents . . .
And, in the meantime, please to accept this poor acknowledgment of
your kindest hospitality.'

So saying, he placed before his humble host a purse of gold *ryo*. But
the old man, after many prostrations, gently pushed back the gift,
and said: 'Kind master, the gold would be of no use to us; and you
will probably have need of it during your long, cold journey. Here
we buy nothing; and we could not spend so much money upon
ourselves, even if we wished . . . As for the girl, we have already
bestowed her as a free gift – she belongs to you: therefore it is not
necessary to ask our leave to take her away. Already she has told us
that she hopes to accompany you, and to remain your servant for as
long as you may be willing to endure her presence. We are only too

happy to know that you deign to accept her; and we pray that you will not trouble yourself on our account. In this place we could not provide her with proper clothing – much less with a dowry. Moreover, being old, we should in any event have to separate from her before long. Therefore it is very fortunate that you should be willing to take her with you now.'

It was in vain that Tomotada tried to persuade the old people to accept a present: he found that they cared nothing for money. But he saw that they were really anxious to trust their daughter's fate to his hands; and he therefore decided to take her with him. So he placed her upon his horse, and bade the old folks farewell for the time being, with many sincere expressions of gratitude.

'Honoured Sir,' the father made answer, 'it is we, and not you, who have reason for gratitude. We are sure that you will be kind to our girl; and we have no fears for her sake.'

[. . .]

[Here, in the Japanese original, there is a queer break in the natural course of the narration, which therefrom remains curiously inconsistent. Nothing further is said about the mother of Tomotada, or about the parents of Aoyagi, or about the daimyo of Noto. Evidently the writer wearied of his work at this point, and hurried the story, very carelessly, to its startling end. I am not able to supply his omissions, or to repair his faults of construction; but I must venture to put in a few explanatory details, without which the rest of the tale would not hold together . . . It appears that Tomotada rashly took Aoyagi with him to Kyoto, and so got into trouble; but we are not informed as to where the couple lived afterwards.]

[. . .]

Now a samurai was not allowed to marry without the consent of his lord; and Tomotada could not expect to obtain this sanction before his mission had been accomplished. He had reason, under such circumstances, to fear that the beauty of Aoyagi might attract dangerous attention, and that means might be devised of taking her away from him. In Kyoto he therefore tried to keep her hidden from curious eyes. But a retainer of Lord Hosokawa one day caught sight of Aoyagi, discovered her relation to Tomotada, and reported the matter to the daimyo. Thereupon the daimyo – a young prince, and fond of pretty faces – gave orders that the girl should be brought to the place; and she was taken thither at once, without ceremony.

Tomotada sorrowed unspeakably; but he knew himself powerless. He was only an humble messenger in the service of a far-off daimyo; and for the time being he was at the mercy of a much more powerful daimyo, whose wishes were not to be questioned. Moreover Tomotada knew that he had acted foolishly – that he had brought about his own misfortune, by entering into a clandestine relation which the code of the military class condemned. There was now but one hope for him – a desperate hope: that Aoyagi might be able and willing to escape and to flee with him. After long reflection, he resolved to try to send her a letter. The attempt would be dangerous, of course: any writing sent to her might find its way to the hands of the daimyo; and to send a love-letter to any inmate of the palace was an unpardonable offence. But he resolved to dare the risk; and, in the form of a Chinese poem, he composed a letter which he endeavoured to have conveyed to her. The poem was written with only twenty-eight characters. But with those twenty-eight characters he was about to express all the depth of his passion, and to suggest all the pain of his loss:[1]

> Koshi o-son gojin wo ou;
> Ryokuju namida wo tarete rakin wo hitataru;
> Komon hitotabi irite fukaki koto umi no gotoshi;
> Kore yori shoro kore rojin

[Closely, closely the youthful prince now follows after the
                                        gem-bright maid –
The tears of the fair one, falling, have moistened all her robes.
But the august lord, having one become enamoured of her –
the depth of his longing is like the depth of the sea.
Therefore it is only I that am left forlorn – only I that am left
                                        to wander alone.]

On the evening of the day after this poem had been sent, Tomotada was summoned to appear before the Lord Hosokawa. The youth at once suspected that his confidence had been betrayed; and he could not hope, if his letter had been seen by the daimyo, to escape the

[1] So the Japanese story-teller would have us believe – although the verses seem commonplace in translation. I have tried to give only their general meaning: an effective literal translation would require some scholarship.

severest penalty. 'Now he will order my death,' thought Tomotada – 'but I do not care to live unless Aoyagi be restored to me. Besides, if the death-sentence be passed, I can at least try to kill Hosokawa.' He slipped his swords into his girdle, and hastened to the palace.

On entering the presence-room he saw the Lord Hosokawa seated upon the daïs, surrounded by samurai of high rank, in caps and robes of ceremony. All were silent as statues; and while Tomotada advanced to make obeisance, the hush seemed to him sinister and heavy, like the stillness before a storm. But Hosokawa suddenly descended from the daïs, and, while taking the youth by the arm, began to repeat the words of the poem '*Koshi o-son gojin wo ou*' . . . And Tomotada, looking up, saw kindly tears in the prince's eyes.

Then said Hosokawa: 'Because you love each other so much, I have taken it upon myself to authorise your marriage, in lieu of my kinsman, the Lord of Noto; and your wedding shall now be celebrated before me. The guests are assembled – the gifts are ready.'

At a signal from the lord, the sliding-screens concealing a further apartment were pushed open; and Tomotada saw there many dignitaries of the court, assembled for the ceremony, and Aoyagi awaiting him in bride's apparel . . . Thus was she given back to him – and the wedding was joyous and splendid – and precious gifts were made to the young couple by the prince, and by the members of his household.

*   *   *

For five happy years, after that wedding, Tomotada and Aoyagi dwelt together. But one morning Aoyagi, while talking with her husband about some household matter, suddenly uttered a great cry of pain, and then became very white and still. After a few moments she said, in a feeble voice: 'Pardon me for thus rudely crying out – but the paid was so sudden! . . . My dear husband, our union must have been brought about through some Karma-relation in a former state of existence; and that happy relation, I think, will bring us again together in more than one life to come. But for this present existence of ours, the relation is now ended – we are about to be separated. Repeat for me, I beseech you, the *Nembutsu*-prayer – because I am dying.'

'Oh! what strange wild fancies!' cried the startled husband – 'you are only a little unwell, my dear one! . . . lie down for a while, and rest; and the sickness will pass . . .'

'No, no!' she responded – 'I am dying! – I do not imagine it – I know! . . . And it were needless now, my dear husband, to hide the truth from you any longer: I am not a human being. The soul of a tree is my soul – the heart of a tree is my heart – the sap of the willow is my life. And someone, at this cruel moment, is cutting down my tree – that is why I must die! . . . Even to weep were now beyond my strength! – Quickly, quickly repeat the *Nembutsu* for me . . . quickly! . . . Ah! . . .

With another cry of pain she turned aside her beautiful head, and tried to hide her face behind her sleeve. But almost in the same moment her whole form appeared to collapse in the strangest way, and to sink down, down, down – level with the floor. Tomotada had sprung to support her – but there was nothing to support! There lay on the matting only the empty robes of the fair creature and the ornaments that she had worn in her hair: the body had ceased to exist . . .

Tomotada shaved his head, took the Buddhist vows, and became an itinerant priest. He travelled through all the provinces of the empire; and, at holy places which he visited, he offered up prayers for the soul of Aoyagi. Reaching Echizen, in the course of his pilgrimage, he sought the home of the parents of his beloved. But when he arrived at the lonely place among the hills, where their dwelling had been, he found that the cottage had disappeared. There was nothing to mark even the spot where it had stood, except the stumps of three willows – two old trees and one young tree – that had been cut down long before his arrival.

Beside the stumps of those willow-trees he erected a memorial tomb, inscribed with divers holy texts; and he there performed many Buddhist services on behalf of the spirits of Aoyagi and of her parents.

JIU-ROKU-ZAKURA

Jiu-roku-zakura

Uso no yona –
Jiu-roku-zakura
Saki ni keri!

In Wakegori, a district of the province of Iyo,[1] there is a very ancient and famous cherry-tree, called *Jiu-roku-zakura*, or 'the Cherry-tree of the Sixteenth Day', because it blooms every year upon the six-teenth day of the first month (by the old lunar calendar) – and only upon that day. Thus the time of its flowering is the Period of Great Cold – though the natural habit of a cherry-tree is to wait for the spring season before venturing to blossom. But the *Jiu-roku-zakura* blossoms with a life that is not – or, at least, that was not originally – its own. There is the ghost of a man in that tree.

He was a samurai of Iyo; and the tree grew in his garden; and it used to flower at the usual time – that is to say, about the end of March or the beginning of April. He had played under that tree when he was a child; and his parents and grandparents and ancestors had hung to its blossoming branches, season after season for more than a hundred years, bright strips of coloured paper inscribed with poems of praise. He himself became very old – outliving all his children; and there was nothing in the world left for him to love except that tree. And lo! in the summer of a certain year, the tree withered and died!

Exceedingly the old man sorrowed for his tree. Then kind neigh-bours found for him a young and beautiful cherry tree, and planted it in his garden – hoping thus to comfort him. And he thanked them, and pretended to be glad. But really his heart was full of pain; for he had loved the old tree so well that nothing could have consoled him for the loss of it.

At last there came to him a happy thought: he remembered a way by which the perishing tree might be saved. (It was the sixteenth day of the first month.) Along he went into his garden, and bowed down

---

1 Present-day Ehime Prefecture.

before the withered tree, and spoke to it, saying: 'Now deign, I beseech you, once more to bloom – because I am going to die in your stead.' (For it is believed that one can really give away one's life to another person, or to a creature or even to a tree, by the favour of the gods – and thus to transfer one's life is expressed by the term *migawari ni tatsu*, 'to act as a substitute'.) Then under that tree he spread a white cloth, and divers coverings, and sat down upon the coverings, and performed *hara-kiri* after the fashion of a samurai. And the ghost of him went into the tree, and made it blossom in that same hour.

And every year it still blooms on the sixteenth day of the first month, in the season of snow.

THE DREAM OF AKINOSUKE

The Dream of Akinosuke

In the district called Toichi of Yamato Province,[1] there used to live a goshi named Miyata Akinosuke . . . [Here I must tell you that in Japanese feudal times there was a privileged class of soldier-farmers – freeholders – corresponding to the class of yeomen in England; and these were called goshi.]

In Akinosuke's garden there was a great and ancient cedar-tree, under which he was wont to rest on sultry days. One very warm afternoon he was sitting under this tree with two of his friends, fellow-goshi, chatting and drinking wine, when he felt all of a sudden very drowsy – so drowsy that he begged his friends to excuse him for taking a nap in their presence. Then he lay down at the foot of the tree, and dreamed this dream.

He thought that as he was lying there in his garden, he saw a procession, like the train of some great daimyo descending a hill near by, and that he got up to look at it. A very grand procession it proved to be – more imposing than anything of the kind which he had ever seen before; and it was advancing toward his dwelling. He observed in the van of it a number of young men richly apparelled, who were drawing a great lacquered palace-carriage, or *gosho-guruma*, hung with bright blue silk. When the procession arrived within a short distance of the house it halted; and a richly dressed man – evidently a person of rank – advanced from it, approached Akinosuke, bowed to him profoundly, and then said: 'Honoured Sir, you see before you a *kerai* [vassal] of the Kokuo of Tokoyo.[2] My master, the King, commands me to greet you in his august name, and to place myself wholly at your disposal. He also bids me inform you that he augustly desires

1 Present-day Nara Prefecture.
2 This name 'Tokoyo' is indefinite. According to circumstances it may signify any unknown country – or that undiscovered country from whose bourn no traveller returns – or that Fairyland of far-eastern fable, the Realm of Horai. The term 'Kokuo' means the ruler of a country – therefore a king. The original phrase, Tokoyo no Kokuo, might be rendered here as 'the Ruler of Horai,' or 'the King of Fairyland'.

your presence at the palace. Be therefore pleased immediately to enter this honourable carriage, which he sent for your conveyance.'

Upon hearing these words Akinosuke wanted to make some fitting reply; but he was too much astonished and embarrassed for speech – and in the same moment his will seemed to melt away from him, so that he could only do as the *kerai* bade him. He entered the carriage; the *kerai* took a place beside him, and made a signal; the drawers, seizing the silken ropes, turned the great vehicle southward – and the journey began.

In a very short time, to Akinosuke's amazement, the carriage stopped in front of a huge two-storeyed gateway (*romon*), of a Chinese style, which he had never before seen. Here the *kerai* dismounted, saying, 'I go to announced the honourable arrival' – and he disappeared. After some little waiting, Akinosuke saw two noble-looking men, wearing robes of purple silk and high caps of the form indicating lofty rank, come from the gateway. These, after having respectfully saluted him, helped him to descend from the carriage, and led him through the great gate and across a vast garden, to the entrance of a palace whose front appeared to extend, west and east, to a distance of miles. Akinosuke was then shown into a reception-room of wonderful size and splendour. His guides conducted him to the place of honour, and respectfully seated themselves apart; while serving-maids, in costume of ceremony, brought refreshments. When Akinosuke had partaken of the refreshments, the two purple-robed attendants bowed low before him, and addressed him in the following words – each speaking alternately, according to the etiquette of courts.

'It is now our honourable duty to inform you . . . as to the reason of your having been summoned hither . . . Our master, the King, augustly desires that you become his son-in-law; . . . and it is his wish and command that you shall wed this very day . . . the August Princess, his maiden-daughter . . . We shall soon conduct you to the presence-chamber . . . where His Augustness even now is waiting to receive you . . . But it will be necessary that we first invest you . . . with the appropriate garments of ceremony.'[1]

Having thus spoken, the attendants rose together, and proceeded to an alcove containing a great chest of gold lacquer. They opened the chest, and took from it various robes and girdles of rich material, and a *kamuri*, or regal headdress. With these they attired Akinosuke

[1] The last phrase, according to old custom, had to be uttered by both attendants at the same time. All these ceremonial observances can still be studied on the Japanese stage.

as befitted a princely bridegroom; and he was then conducted to the presence-room, where he saw the Kokuo of Tokoyo seated upon the *daiza*,[1] wearing a high black cap of state, and robed in robes of yellow silk. Before the *daiza*, to left and right, a multitude of dignitaries sat in rank, motionless and splendid as images in a temple; and Akinosuke, advancing into their midst, saluted the king with the triple prostration of usage. The king greeted him with gracious words, and then said: 'You have already been informed as to the reason of your having been summoned to Our presence. We have decided that you shall become the adopted husband of Our only daughter – and the wedding ceremony shall now be performed.'

As the king finished speaking, a sound of joyful music was heard; and a long train of beautiful court ladies advanced from behind a curtain to conduct Akinosuke to the room in which the bride awaited him.

The room was immense; but it could scarcely contain the multitude of guests assembled to witness the wedding ceremony. All bowed down before Akinosuke as he took his place, facing the King's daughter, on the kneeling-cushion prepared for him. As a maiden of heaven the bride appeared to be; and her robes were beautiful as a summer sky. And the marriage was performed amid great rejoicing.

Afterwards the pair were conducted to a suite of apartments that had been prepared for them in another portion of the palace; and there they received the congratulations of many noble persons, and wedding gifts beyond counting.

Some days later Akinosuke was again summoned to the throne-room. On this occasion he was received even more graciously than before; and the King said to him: 'In the south-western part of Our dominion there is an island called Raishu. We have now appointed you Governor of that island. You will find the people loyal and docile; but their laws have not yet been brought into proper accord with the laws of Tokoyo; and their customs have not been properly regulated. We entrust you with the duty of improving their social condition as far as may be possible; and We desire that you shall rule them with kindness and wisdom. All preparations necessary for your journey to Raishu have already been made.'

---

1 This was the name given to the estrade, or daïs, upon which a feudal prince or ruler sat in state. The term literally signifies 'great seat'.

So Akinosuke and his bride departed from the palace of Tokoyo, accompanied to the shore by a great escort of nobles and officials; and they embarked upon a ship of state provided by the king. And with favouring winds they safely sailed to Raishu, and found the good people of that island assembled upon the beach to welcome them.

Akinosuke entered at once upon his new duties; and they did not prove to be hard. During the first three years of his governorship he was occupied chiefly with the framing and the enactment of laws; but he had wise counsellors to help him, and he never found the work unpleasant. When it was all finished, he had no active duties to perform, beyond attending the rites and ceremonies ordained by ancient custom. The country was so healthy and so fertile that sickness and want were unknown; and the people were so good that no laws were ever broken. And Akinosuke dwelt and ruled in Raishu for twenty years more – making in all twenty-three years of sojourn, during which no shadow of sorrow traversed his life.

But in the twenty-fourth year of his governorship, a great misfortune came upon him; for his wife, who had borne him seven children – five boys and two girls – fell sick and died. She was buried, with high pomp, on the summit of a beautiful hill in the district of Hanryoko; and a monument, exceedingly splendid, was placed upon her grave. But Akinosuke felt such grief at her death that he no longer cared to live.

Now when the legal period of mourning was over, there came to Raishu, from the Tokoyo palace, a *shisha*, or royal messenger. The *shisha* delivered to Akinosuke a message of condolence, and then said to him: 'These are the words which our august master, the King of Tokoyo, commands that I repeat to you: "We will now send you back to your own people and country. As for the seven children, they are the grandsons and granddaughters of the King, and shall be fitly cared for. Do not, therefore, allow your mind to be troubled concerning them." '

On receiving this mandate, Akinosuke submissively prepared for his departure. When all his affairs had been settled, and the ceremony of bidding farewell to his counsellors and trusted officials had been concluded, he was escorted with much honour to the port. There he embarked upon the ship sent for him; and the ship sailed out into the blue sea, under the blue sky; and the shape of the island of Raishu itself turned blue, and then turned grey, and then vanished forever . . . And Akinosuke suddenly awoke – under the cedar-tree in his own garden!

For a moment he was stupefied and dazed. But he perceived his two friends still seated near him – drinking and chatting merrily. He stared at them in a bewildered way, and cried aloud: 'How strange!'

'Akinosuke must have been dreaming,' one of them exclaimed, with a laugh. 'What did you see, Akinosuke, that was strange?'

Then Akinosuke told his dream – that dream of three-and-twenty years' sojourn in the realm of Tokoyo, in the island of Raishu – and they were astonished, because he had really slept for no more than a few minutes.

One goshi said: 'Indeed, you saw strange things. We also saw something strange while you were napping. A little yellow butterfly was fluttering over your face for a moment or two; and we watched it. Then it alighted on the ground beside you, close to the tree; and almost as soon as it alighted there, a big, big ant came out of a hole and seized it and pulling it down into the hole. Just before you woke up, we saw that very butterfly come out of the hole again, and flutter over your face as before. And then it suddenly disappeared: we do not know where it went.'

'Perhaps it was Akinosuke's soul,' the other goshi said – 'certainly I thought I saw it fly into his mouth . . . But, even if that butterfly *was* Akinosuke's soul, the fact would not explain his dream.'

'The ants might explain it,' returned the first speaker. 'Ants are queer beings – possibly goblins . . . Anyhow, there is a big ant's nest under that cedar-tree . . . '

'Let us look!' cried Akinosuke, greatly moved by this suggestion. And he went for a spade.

The ground about and beneath the cedar-tree proved to have been excavated, in a most surprising way, by a prodigious colony of ants. The ants had furthermore built inside their excavations; and their tiny constructions of straw, clay, and stems bore an odd resemblance to miniature towns. In the middle of a structure considerably larger than the rest there was a marvellous swarming of small ants around the body of one very big ant, which had yellowish wings and a long black head.

'Why, there is the King of my dream!' cried Akinosuke; 'and there is the palace of Tokoyo! . . . How extraordinary! . . . Raishu ought to lie somewhere south-west of it – to the left of that big root . . . Yes! –

here it is! . . . How very strange! Now I am sure that I can find the mountain of Hanryoko, and the grave of the princess . . . '

In the wreck of the nest he searched and searched, and at last discovered a tiny mound, on the top of which was fixed a water-worn pebble, in shape resembling a Buddhist monument. Underneath it he found – embedded in clay – the dead body of a female ant.

RIKI-BAKA

Riki-Baka

His name was Riki, signifying Strength; but the people called him Riki-the-Simple, or Riki-the-Fool – 'Riki-Baka' – because he had been born into perpetual childhood. For the same reason they were kind to him – even when he set a house on fire by putting a lighted match to a mosquito-curtain, and clapped his hands for joy to see the blaze. At sixteen years he was a tall, strong lad; but in mind he remained always at the happy age of two, and therefore continued to play with very small children. The bigger children of the neighbourhood, from four to seven years old, did not care to play with him, because he could not learn their songs and games. His favourite toy was a broomstick, which he used as a hobby-horse; and for hours at a time he would ride on that broomstick, up and down the slope in front of my house, with amazing peals of laughter. But at last he became troublesome by reason of his noise; and I had to tell him that he must find another playground. He bowed submissively, and then went off – sorrowfully trailing his broomstick behind him. Gentle at all times, and perfectly harmless if allowed no chance to play with fire, he seldom gave anybody cause for complaint. His relation to the life of our street was scarcely more than that of a dog or a chicken; and when he finally disappeared, I did not miss him. Months and months passed by before anything happened to remind me of Riki.

'What has become of Riki?' I then asked the old woodcutter who supplies our neighbourhood with fuel. I remembered that Riki had often helped him to carry his bundles.

'Riki-Baka?' answered the old man. 'Ah, Riki is dead – poor fellow! . . . Yes, he died nearly a year ago, very suddenly; the doctors said that he had some disease of the brain. And there is a strange story now about that poor Riki.

'When Riki died, his mother wrote his name, "Riki-Baka", in the palm of his left hand – putting "Riki" in the Chinese character, and "Baka" in *kana*.[1] And she repeated many prayers for him – prayers that he might be reborn into some more happy condition.

1 *Kana*: the Japanese phonetic alphabet.

'Now, about three months ago, in the honourable residence of Nanigashi-Sama,[1] in Kojimachi,[2] a boy was born with characters on the palm of his left hand; and the characters were quite plain to read – "RIKI-BAKA"!

'So the people of that house knew that the birth must have happened in answer to somebody's prayer; and they caused inquiry to be made everywhere. At last a vegetable-seller brought word to them that there used to be a simple lad, called Riki-Baka, living in the Ushigome quarter, and that he had died during the last autumn; and they sent two men-servants to look for the mother of Riki.

'Those servants found the mother of Riki, and told her what had happened; and she was glad exceedingly – for that Nanigashi house is a very rich and famous house. But the servants said that the family of Nanigashi-Sama were very angry about the word "Baka" on the child's hand. "And where is your Riki buried?" the servants asked. "He is buried in the cemetery of Zendoji," she told them. "Please to give us some of the clay of his grave," they requested.

'So she went with them to the temple Zendoji, and showed them Riki's grave; and they took some of the grave-clay away with them, wrapped up in a *furoshiki* [3] . . . They gave Riki's mother some money – ten yen [4]. . . '

'But what did they want with that clay?' I inquired.

'Well,' the old man answered, 'you know that it would not do to let the child grow up with that name on his hand. And there is no other means of removing characters that come in that way upon the body of a child: *you must rub the skin with clay taken from the grave of the body of the former birth* . . . '

---

1 'So-and-so': appellation used by Hearn in place of the real name.
2 A section of Tokyo.
3 A square piece of cotton-goods, or other woven material, used as a wrapper in which to carry small packages.
4 Ten yen is nothing now, but was a formidable sum then.

HI-MAWARI

Hi-Mawari

On the wooded hill behind the house Robert and I are looking for fairy-rings. Robert is eight years old, comely, and very wise – I am a little more than seven – and I reverence Robert. It is a glowing glorious August day; and the warm air is filled with sharp sweet scents of resin.

We do not find any fairy-rings; but we find a great many pine-cones in the high grass . . . I tell Robert the old Welsh story of the man who went to sleep, unawares, inside a fairy-ring, and so disappeared for seven years, and would never eat or speak after his friends had delivered him from the enchantment.

'They eat nothing but the points of needles, you know,' says Robert.

'Who?' I ask.

"Goblins,' Robert answers.

This revelation leaves me dumb with astonishment and awe . . . But Robert suddenly cries out: 'There is a Harper! – he is coming to the house!'

And down the hill we run to hear the harper . . . But what a harper! Not like the hoary minstrels of the picture-books. A swarthy, sturdy, unkempt vagabond, with black bold eyes under scowling black brows. More like a bricklayer than a bard – and his garments are corduroy!

'Wonder if he is going to sing in Welsh?' murmurs Robert.

I feel too much disappointed to make any remarks. The harper poses his harp – a huge instrument – upon our doorstep, sets all the strings ringing with a sweep of his grimy fingers, clears his throat with a sort of angry growl, and begins –

> Believe me, if all those endearing young charms,
> Which I gaze on so fondly today . . .

The accent, the attitude, the voice, all fill me with repulsion unutterable – shock me with a new sensation of formidable vulgarity. I want to cry out loud, 'You have no right to sing that song!' For I have heard it sung by the lips of the dearest and fairest being in my little world – and that this rude, coarse man should dare to sing it vexes me like a mockery – angers me like an insolence. But only for a moment! . . . With the utterance of the syllables 'today', that deep, grim voice suddenly breaks into a quivering tenderness indescribable – then, marvellously changing, it mellows into tones sonorous and rich as the bass of a great organ – while a sensation unlike anything ever felt before takes me by the throat . . . What witchcraft has he learned? What secret has he found – this scowling man of the road? . . . Oh! is there anybody else in the whole world who can sing like that? . . . And the form of the singer flickers and dims – and the house, and the lawn, and all visible shapes of things tremble and swim before me. Yet instinctively I fear that man – I almost hate him; and I feel myself flushing with anger and shame because of his power to move me thus . . .

'He made you cry,' Robert compassionately observes, to my further confusion – as the harper strides away, richer by a gift of sixpence taken without thanks . . . 'But I think he must be a gypsy. Gypsies are bad people – and they are wizards . . . Let us go back to the wood.'

We climb again to the pines, and there squat down upon the sun-flecked grass, and look over town and sea. But we do not play as before: the spell of the wizard is strong upon us both . . . 'Perhaps he is a goblin,' I venture at last, 'or a fairy?'

'No,' says Robert – 'only a gypsy. But that is nearly as bad. They steal children, you know . . . '

'What shall we do if he comes up here?' I gasp, in sudden terror at the lonesomeness of our situation.

'Oh, he wouldn't dare,' answers Robert – 'not by daylight, you know . . . '

[Only yesterday, near the village of Takata, I noticed a flower which the Japanese call by nearly the same name as we do: *Himawari*, 'The Sunward-turning' – and over the space of forty years there thrilled back to me the voice of that wandering harper –

> *As the Sunflower turns on her god, when he sets,*
> *The same look that she turned when he rose.*

Again I saw the sun-flecked shadows on that far Welsh hill; and Robert for a moment again stood beside me, with his girl's face and his curls of gold. We were looking for fairy-rings . . . But all that existed of the real Robert must long ago have suffered a sea-change into something rich and strange . . . Greater love hath no man than this, that a man lay down his life for his friend . . .]

HORAI

Horai

Blue vision of depth lost in height – sea and sky interblending through luminous haze. The day is of spring, and the hour morning.

Only sky and sea – one azure enormity . . . In the fore, ripples are catching a silvery light, and threads of foam are swirling. But a little further off no motion is visible, nor anything save colour: dim warm blue of water widening away to melt into blue of air. Horizon there is none: only distance soaring into space – infinite concavity hollowing before you, and hugely arching above you – the colour deepening with the height. But far in the midway-blue there hangs a faint, faint vision of palace towers, with high roofs horned and curved like moons – some shadowing of splendour strange and old, illumined by a sunshine soft as memory.

. . . What I have thus been trying to describe is a *kakemono* – that is to say, a Japanese painting on silk, suspended to the wall of my alcove – and the name of it is *Shinkiro*, which signifies 'Mirage'. But the shapes of the mirage are unmistakable. Those are the glimmering portals of Horai the blest; and those are the moony roofs of the Palace of the Dragon-King – and the fashion of them (though limned by a Japanese brush of today) is the fashion of things Chinese, twenty-one hundred years ago . . .

Thus much is told of the place in the Chinese books of that time –

In Horai there is neither death nor pain; and there is no winter. The flowers in that place never fade, and the fruits never fail; and if a man taste of those fruits even but once, he can never again feel thirst or hunger. In Horai grow the enchanted plants *So-rin-shi*, and *Riku-go-aoi*, and *Ban-kon-to*, which heal all manner of sickness – and there grows also the magical grass *Yo-shin-shi*, that quickens the dead; and the magical grass is watered by a fairy water of which a single drink confers perpetual youth. The people of Horai eat their rice out of very, very small bowls; but the rice never diminishes within those bowls – however much of it be eaten – until the eater desires no more. And the people of Horai drink their wine out of very, very small cups; but no man can empty one of those cups – however stoutly he may drink – until there comes upon him the pleasant drowsiness of intoxication.

All this and more is told in the legends of the time of the Shin dynasty. But that the people who wrote down those legends ever saw Horai, even in a mirage, is not believable. For really there are no enchanted fruits which leave the eater forever satisfied – nor any magical grass which revives the dead – nor any fountain of fairy water – nor any bowls which never lack rice – nor any cups which never lack wine. It is not true that sorrow and death never enter Horai – neither is it true that there is not any winter. The winter in Horai is cold – and winds then bite to the bone; and the heaping of snow is monstrous on the roofs of the Dragon-King.

Nevertheless there are wonderful things in Horai; and the most wonderful of all has not been mentioned by any Chinese writer. I mean the atmosphere of Horai. It is an atmosphere peculiar to the place; and, because of it, the sunshine in Horai is *whiter* than any other sunshine – a milky light that never dazzles – astonishingly clear, but very soft. This atmosphere is not of our human period: it is enormously old – so old that I feel afraid when I try to think how old it is – and it is not a mixture of nitrogen and oxygen. It is not made of air at all, but of ghost – the substance of quintillions of quintillions of generations of souls blended into one immense translucency – souls of people who thought in ways never resembling our ways. Whatever mortal man inhales that atmosphere, he takes into his blood the thrilling of these spirits; and they change the sense within him – reshaping his notions of Space and Time – so that he can see only as they used to see, and feel only as they used to feel, and think only as they used to think. Soft as sleep are these changes of sense; and Horai, discerned across them, might thus be described:

– *Because in Horai there is no knowledge of great evil, the hearts of the people never grow old. And, by reason of being always young in heart, the people of Horai smile from birth until death – except when the gods send sorrow among them; and faces then are veiled until the sorrow goes away. All folk in Horai love and trust each other, as if all were members of a single household – and the speech of the women is like birdsong, because the hearts of them are light as the souls of birds – and the swaying of the sleeves of the maidens at play seems a flutter of wide, soft wings. In Horai nothing is hidden but grief, because there is no reason for shame – and nothing is locked away, because there could not be any theft – and by night as well as by day all doors remain unbarred, because there is no reason for fear. And because the people are fairies – though mortal – all things in Horai, except the Palace of the Dragon-King, are small and quaint and queer – and these fairy-folk do really eat their rice out of very, very small bowls, and drink their wine out of very, very small cups . . .*

– Much of this seeming would be due to the inhalation of that ghostly atmosphere – but not all. For the spell wrought by the dead is only the charm of an Ideal, the glamour of an ancient hope – and something of that hope has found fulfilment in many hearts – in the simple beauty of unselfish lives – in the sweetness of Woman . . .

– Evil winds from the West are blowing over Horai; and the magical atmosphere, alas! is shrinking away before them. It lingers now in patches only, and bands – like those long bright bands of cloud that train across the landscapes of Japanese painters. Under these shreds of the elfish vapour you still can find Horai – but not everywhere . . . Remember that Horai is also called *Shinkiro*, which signifies Mirage – the Vision of the Intangible. And the Vision is fading – never again to appear save in pictures and poems and dreams . . .

IN GHOSTLY JAPAN

FRAGMENT

Yoru bakari
Miru mono nari to
Omou-nayo!
Hiru sae yume no
Ukiyo nari-keri.

Think not that dreams
    appear to the dreamer
      only at night:
The dream of this world of pain
    appears to us
      even by day.

Fragment

[. . .]

And it was at the hour of sunset that they came to the foot of the mountain. There was in that place no sign of life – neither token of water, nor trace of plant, nor shadow of flying bird – nothing but desolation rising to desolation. And the summit was lost in heaven.

Then the Bodhisattva said to his young companion: 'What you have asked to see will be shown to you. But the place of the Vision is far; and the way is rude. Follow after me, and do not fear: strength will be given you.'

Twilight gloomed about them as they climbed. There was no beaten path, nor any mark of former human visitation; and the way was over an endless heaping of tumbled fragments that rolled or turned beneath the foot. Sometimes a mass dislodged would clatter down with hollow echoings – sometimes the substance trodden would burst like an empty shell . . . Stars pointed and thrilled; and the darkness deepened.

'Do not fear, my son,' said the Bodhisattva, guiding: 'danger there is none, though the way be grim.'

Under the stars they climbed – fast, fast – mounting by help of power superhuman. High zones of mist they passed; and they saw below them, ever widening as they climbed, a soundless flood of cloud, like the tide of a milky sea.

Hour after hour they climbed – and forms invisible yielded to their tread with dull soft crashings – and faint cold fires lighted and died at every breaking.

And once the pilgrim-youth laid hand on a something smooth that was not stone – and lifted it – and dimly saw the cheekless gibe of death.

'Linger not thus, my son!' urged the voice of the teacher – 'the summit that we must gain is very far away!'

On through the dark they climbed – and felt continually beneath them the soft strange breakings – and saw the icy fires worm and die – till the rim of the night turned grey, and the stars began to fail, and the east began to bloom.

Yet still they climbed – fast, fast – mounting by help of power superhuman. About them now was frigidness of death – and silence tremendous . . . A gold flame kindled in the east.

Then first to the pilgrim's gaze the steeps revealed their nakedness – and a trembling seized him – and a ghastly fear. For there was not any ground – neither beneath him nor about him nor above him – but a heaping only, monstrous and measureless, of skulls and fragments of skulls and dust of bone – with a shimmer of shed teeth strewn through the drift of it, like the shimmer of scrags of shell in the wrack of a tide.

'Do not fear, my son!' cried the voice of the Bodhisattva – 'only the strong of heart can win to the place of the Vision!'

Behind them the world had vanished. Nothing remained but the clouds beneath, and the sky above, and the heaping of skulls between – up-slanting out of sight.

Then the sun climbed with the climbers; and there was no warmth in the light of him, but coldness sharp as a sword. And the horror of stupendous height, and the nightmare of stupendous depth, and the terror of silence, ever grew and grew, and weighed upon the pilgrim, and held his feet – so that suddenly all power departed from him, and he moaned like a sleeper in dreams.

'Hasten, hasten, my son!' cried the Bodhisattva: 'the day is brief, and the summit is very far away.'

But the pilgrim shrieked – 'I fear! I fear unspeakably! – and the power has departed from me!'

'The power will return, my son,' made answer the Bodhisattva . . . 'Look now below you and above you and about you, and tell me what you see.'

'I cannot,' cried the pilgrim, trembling and clinging; 'I dare not look beneath! Before me and about me there is nothing but skulls of men.'

'And yet, my son,' said the Bodhisattva, laughing softly – 'and yet you do not know of what this mountain is made.'

The other, shuddering, repeated: 'I fear! – Unutterably I fear! . . . there is nothing but skulls of men!'

'A mountain of skulls it is,' responded the Bodhisattva. 'But know, my son, that all of them *are your own*! Each has at some time been the nest of your dreams and delusions and desires. Not even one of them is the skull of any other being. All – all without exception – have been yours, in the billions of your former lives.'

FURISODE

Furisode

Recently, while passing through a little street tenanted chiefly by dealers in old wares, I noticed a *furisode*, or long-sleeved robe, of the rich purple tint called *murasaki*, hanging before one of the shops. It was a robe such as might have been worn by a lady of rank in the time of the Tokugawa. I stopped to look at the five crests upon it; and in the same moment there came to my recollection this legend of a similar robe said to have once caused the destruction of Yedo.

Nearly two hundred and fifty years ago, the daughter of a rich merchant of the city of the Shoguns, while attending some temple-festival, perceived in the crowd a young samurai of remarkable beauty, and immediately fell in love with him. Unhappily for her, he disappeared in the press before she could learn through her attendants who he was or whence he had come. But his image remained vivid in her memory – even to the least detail of his costume. The holiday attire then worn by samurai youths was scarcely less brilliant than that of young girls; and the upper dress of this handsome stranger had seemed wonderfully beautiful to the enamoured maiden. She fancied that by wearing a robe of like quality and colour, bearing the same crest, she might be able to attract his notice on some future occasion.

Accordingly she had such a robe made, with very long sleeves, according to the fashion of the period; and she prized it greatly. She wore it whenever she went out; and when at home she would suspend it in her room, and try to imagine the form of her unknown beloved within it. Sometimes she would pass hours before it – dreaming and weeping by turns. And she would pray to the gods and the Buddhas that she might win the young man's affection – often repeating the invocation of the Nichiren sect: *Namu myo ho renge kyo!*

But she never saw the youth again; and she pined with longing for him, and sickened, and died, and was buried. After her burial, the long-sleeved robe that she had so much prized was given to the Buddhist temple of which her family were parishioners. It is an old custom to thus dispose of the garments of the dead.

The priest was able to sell the robe at a good price; for it was a costly silk, and bore no trace of the tears that had fallen upon it. It was bought by a girl of about the same age as the dead lady. She wore it only one day. Then she fell sick, and began to act strangely – crying out that she was haunted by the vision of a beautiful young man, and that for love of him she was going to die. And within a little while she died; and the long-sleeved robe was a second time presented to the temple.

Again the priest sold it; and again it became the property of a young girl, who wore it only once. Then she also sickened, and talked of a beautiful shadow, and died, and was buried. And the robe was given a third time to the temple; and the priest wondered and doubted.

Nevertheless he ventured to sell the luckless garment once more. Once more it was purchased by a girl and once more worn; and the wearer pined and died. And the robe was given a fourth time to the temple.

Then the priest felt sure that there was some evil influence at work; and he told his acolytes to make a fire in the temple-court, and to burn the robe.

So they made a fire, into which the robe was thrown. But as the silk began to burn, there suddenly appeared upon it dazzling characters of flame – the characters of the invocation, *Namu myo ho renge kyo* – and these, one by one, leaped like great sparks to the temple roof; and the temple took fire.

Embers from the burning temple presently dropped upon neighbouring roofs; and the whole street was soon ablaze. Then a sea wind, rising, blew destruction into further streets; and the conflagration spread from street to street, and from district into district, till nearly the whole of the city was consumed. And this calamity, which occurred upon the eighteenth day of the first month of the first year of Meireki (1655), is still remembered in Tokyo as the *Furisode-Kwaji* – the Great Fire of the Long-sleeved Robe.

According to a story-book called *Kibun-Daijin*, the name of the girl who caused the robe to be made was O-Same; and she was the daughter of Hikoyemon, a wine-merchant of Hyakusho-machi, in the district of Azabu. Because of her beauty she was also called

Azabu-Komachi, or the Komachi of Azabu.[1] The same book says that the temple of the tradition was a Nichiren temple called Hon-myoji, in the district of Hongo; and that the crest upon the robe was a *kikyo*-flower. But there are many different versions of the story; and I distrust the *Kibun-Daijin* because it asserts that the beautiful samurai was not really a man, but a transformed dragon, or water-serpent, that used to inhabit the lake at Uyeno – *Shinobazu-no-Ike*.

[1] After more than a thousand years, the name of Komachi, or Ono-no- Komachi, is still celebrated in Japan. She was the most beautiful woman of her time, and so great a poet that she could move heaven by her verses, and cause rain to fall in time of drought. Many men loved her in vain; and many are said to have died for love of her. But misfortunes visited her when her youth had passed; and, after having been reduced to the uttermost want, she became a beggar, and died at last upon the public highway, near Kyoto. As it was thought shameful to bury her in the foul rags found upon her, some poor person gave a worn-out summer-robe (*katabira*) to wrap her body in; and she was interred near Arashiyama at a spot still pointed out to travellers as the 'Place of the Katabira' (*Katabira-no-Tsuchi*).

INCENSE

Incense

I see, rising out of darkness, a lotos in a vase. Most of the vase is invisible, but I know that it is of bronze, and that its glimpsing handles are bodies of dragons. Only the lotos is fully illuminated: three pure white flowers, and five great leaves of gold and green – gold above, green on the upcurling under-surface – an artificial lotos. It is bathed by a slanting stream of sunshine – the darkness beneath and beyond is the dusk of a temple-chamber. I do not see the opening through which the radiance pours, but I am aware that it is a small window shaped in the outline-form of a temple-bell.

The reason that I see the lotos – one memory of my first visit to a Buddhist sanctuary – is that there has come to me an odour of incense. Often when I smell incense, this vision defines; and usually thereafter other sensations of my first day in Japan revive in swift succession with almost painful acuteness.

It is almost ubiquitous – this perfume of incense. It makes one element of the faint but complex and never-to-be-forgotten odour of the Far East. It haunts the dwelling-house not less than the temple – the home of the peasant not less than the yashiki of the prince. Shinto shrines, indeed, are free from it – incense being an abomination to the elder gods. But wherever Buddhism lives there is incense. In every house containing a Buddhist shrine or Buddhist tablets, incense is burned at certain times; and in even the rudest country solitudes you will find incense smouldering before way-side images – little stone figures of Fudo, Jizo, or Kwannon. Many experiences of travel – strange impressions of sound as well as of sight – remain associated in my own memory with that fragrance: vast silent shadowed avenues leading to weird old shrines – mossed flights of worn steps ascending to temples that moulder above the clouds – joyous tumult of festival nights – sheeted funeral-trains gliding by in glimmer of lanterns; murmur of household prayer in fishermen's huts on far wild coasts – and visions of desolate little

graves marked only by threads of blue smoke ascending – graves of
pet animals or birds remembered by simple hearts in the hour of
prayer to Amida, the Lord of Immeasurable Light.

But the odour of which I speak is that of cheap incense only – the
incense in general use. There are many other kinds of incense; and
the range of quality is amazing. A bundle of common incense-rods –
(they are about as thick as an ordinary pencil-lead, and somewhat
longer) – can be bought for a few sen; while a bundle of better quality,
presenting to inexperienced eyes only some difference in colour,
may cost several yen, and be cheap at the price. Still costlier sorts
of incense – veritable luxuries – take the form of lozenges, wafers,
pastilles; and a small envelope of such material may be worth four
or five pounds sterling. But the commercial and industrial questions
relating to Japanese incense represent the least interesting part of a
remarkably curious subject.

2

Curious indeed, but enormous by reason of its infinity of tradition
and detail. I am afraid even to think of the size of the volume that
would be needed to cover it . . . Such a work would properly begin
with some brief account of the earliest knowledge and use of arom-
atics in Japan. I would next treat of the records and legends of the
first introduction of Buddhist incense from Korea – when King
Shomyo of Kudara, in 551 AD, sent to the island-empire a collection
of sutras, an image of the Buddha, and one complete set of furniture
for a temple. Then something would have to be said about those
classifications of incense which were made during the tenth century,
in the periods of Engi and of Tenryaku – and about the report of
the ancient state-councillor, Kimitaka-Sangi, who visited China in
the latter part of the thirteenth century, and transmitted to the
Emperor Yomei the wisdom of the Chinese concerning incense.
Then mention should be made of the ancient incenses still preserved
in various Japanese temples, and of the famous fragments of *ranjatai*
(publicly exhibited at Nara in the tenth year of Meiji) which furnished supplies to the three great captains, Nobunaga, Hideyoshi, and
Iyeyasu. After this should follow an outline of the history of mixed
incenses made in Japan – with notes on the classifications devised by
the luxurious Takauji, and on the nomenclature established later by
Ashikaga Yoshimasa, who collected one hundred and thirty varieties
of incense, and invented for the more precious of them names
recognised even to this day – such as 'Blossom-Showering', 'Smoke-

of-Fuji' and 'Flower-of-the-Pure-Law'. Examples ought to be given likewise of traditions attaching to historical incenses preserved in several princely families, together with specimens of those hereditary recipes for incense-making which have been transmitted from generation to generation through hundreds of years, and are still called after their august inventors – as 'the Method of Hina-Dainagon', 'the Method of Sento-In', etc. Recipes also should be given of those strange incenses made '*to imitate the perfume of the lotos, the smell of the summer breeze, and the odour of the autumn wind*'. Some legends of the great period of incense-luxury should be cited – such as the story of Suë Owari-no-Kami, who built for himself a palace of incense-woods, and set fire to it on the night of his revolt, when the smoke of its burning perfumed the land to a distance of twelve miles . . . Of course the mere compilation of materials for a history of mixed-incenses would entail the study of a host of documents, treatises, and books – particularly of such strange works as the *Kun-Shu-Rui-Sho*, or 'Incense-Collector's Classifying-Manual' – containing the teachings of the Ten Schools of the Art of Mixing Incense; directions as to the best seasons for incense-making; and instructions about the '*different kinds of fire*' to be used for burning incense – (one kind is called 'literary fire,' and another 'military fire'); together with rules for pressing the ashes of a censer into various artistic designs corresponding to season and occasion . . . A special chapter should certainly be given to the incense-bags (*kusadama*) hung up in houses to drive away goblins – and to the smaller incense-bags formerly carried about the person as a protection against evil spirits. Then a very large part of the work would have to be devoted to the religious uses and legends of incense – a huge subject in itself. There would also have to be considered the curious history of the old 'incense-assemblies', whose elaborate ceremonial could be explained only by help of numerous diagrams. One chapter at least would be required for the subject of the ancient importation of incense-materials from India, China, Annam, Siam, Cambodia, Ceylon, Sumatra, Java, Borneo, and various islands of the Malay archipelago – places all named in rare books about incense. And a final chapter should treat of the romantic literature of incense – the poems, stories, and dramas in which incense-rites are mentioned; and especially those love-songs comparing the body to incense, and passion to the eating flame:

> *Even as burns the perfume lending thy robe its fragrance,*
> *Smoulders my life away, consumed by the pain of longing!*

. . . The merest outline of the subject is terrifying! I shall attempt nothing more than a few notes about the religious, the luxurious, and the ghostly uses of incense.

3

The common incense everywhere burned by poor people before Buddhist icons is called *an-soku-ko*. This is very cheap. Great quantities of it are burned by pilgrims in the bronze censers set before the entrances of famous temples; and in front of roadside images you may often see bundles of it. These are for the use of pious wayfarers, who pause before every Buddhist image on their path to repeat a brief prayer and, when possible, to set a few rods smouldering at the feet of the statue. But in rich temples, and during great religious ceremonies, much more expensive incense is used. Altogether three classes of perfumes are employed in Buddhist rites: *ko*, or incense-proper, in many varieties – (the word literally means only 'fragrant substance') – *dzuko*, an odorous ointment; and *makko*, a fragrant powder. *Ko* is burned; *dzuko* is rubbed upon the hands of the priest as an ointment of purification; and *makko* is sprinkled about the sanctuary. This *makko* is said to be identical with the sandalwood-powder so frequently mentioned in Buddhist texts. But it is only the true incense which can be said to bear an important relation to the religious service.

'Incense,' declares the *Soshi-Ryaku*,[1] 'is the Messenger of Earnest Desire. When the rich Sudatta wished to invite the Buddha to a repast, he made use of incense. He was wont to ascend to the roof of his house on the eve of the day of the entertainment, and to remain standing there all night, holding a censer of precious incense. And as often as he did thus, the Buddha never failed to come on the following day at the exact time desired.'

This text plainly implies that incense, as a burnt-offering, symbolizes the pious desires of the faithful. But it symbolizes other things also; and it has furnished many remarkable similes to Buddhist literature. Some of these, and not the least interesting, occur in prayers, of which the following, from the book called *Hoji-san*[2] is a striking example: '*Let my body remain pure like a censer! – Let my thought be ever as a fire of wisdom, purely consuming the incense of sila and of dhyana,[3] that so may I do homage to all the Buddhas in the Ten Directions of the Past, the Present, and the Future!*'

1 'Short [or Epitomized] History of Priests'.
2 'The Praise of Pious Observances'.
3 By *sila* is meant the observance of the rules of purity in act and thought; *dhyana* (called by Japanese Buddhists *zenjo*) is one of the higher forms of meditation.

Sometimes in Buddhist sermons the destruction of Karma by virtuous effort is likened to the burning of incense by a pure flame – sometimes, again, the life of man is compared to the smoke of incense. In his 'Hundred Writings' (*Hyaku-tsu-kiri-kami*), the Shinshu priest Myoden says, quoting from the Buddhist work *Kujikkajo*, or 'Ninety Articles':

> In the burning of incense we see that so long as any incense remains, so long does the burning continue, and the smoke mount skyward. Now the breath of this body of ours – this impermanent combination of Earth, Water, Air, and Fire – is like that smoke. And the changing of the incense into cold ashes when the flame expires is an emblem of the changing of our bodies into ashes when our funeral pyres have burnt themselves out.

He also tells us about that Incense-Paradise of which every believer ought to be reminded by the perfume of earthly incense:

> In the Thirty-Second Vow for the Attainment of the Paradise of Wondrous Incense [he says] it is written: '*that Paradise is formed of hundreds of thousands of different kinds of incense, and of substances incalculably precious – the beauty of it incomparably exceeds anything in the heavens or in the sphere of man – the fragrance of it perfumes all the worlds of the Ten Directions of Space; and all who perceive that odour practise Buddha-deeds.*' In ancient times there were men of superior wisdom and virtue who, by reason of their vow, obtained perception of the odour; but we, who are born with inferior wisdom and virtue in these later days, cannot obtain such perception. Nevertheless it will be well for us, when we smell the incense kindled before the image of Amida, to imagine that its odour is the wonderful fragrance of Paradise, and to repeat the *Nembutsu* in gratitude for the mercy of the Buddha.

4

But the use of incense in Japan is not confined to religious rites and ceremonies: indeed the costlier kinds of incense are manufactured chiefly for social entertainments. Incense-burning has been an amusement of the aristocracy ever since the thirteenth century. Probably you have heard of the Japanese tea-ceremonies, and their curious Buddhist history; and I suppose that every foreign collector of Japanese bric-a-brac knows something about the luxury to which these ceremonies at one period attained – a luxury well attested by the quality of the beautiful utensils formerly employed in them. But there were, and still are, incense-ceremonies much more elaborate and costly than the tea-ceremonies – and also much more interesting. Besides music, embroidery, poetical composition and other branches of the old-fashioned female education, the young lady of pre-Meiji days was expected to acquire three especially polite accomplishments – the art of arranging flowers (*ikebana*), the art of ceremonial tea-making (*cha-no-yu* or *cha-no-e*),[1] and the etiquette of incense-parties (*ko-kwai* or *ko-e*). Incense-parties were invented before the time of the Ashikaga shoguns, and were most in vogue during the peaceful period of the Tokugawa rule. With the fall of the shogunate they went out of fashion; but recently they have been to some extent revived. It is not likely, however, that they will again become really fashionable in the old sense – partly because they represented rare forms of social refinement that never can be revived, and partly because of their costliness.

In translating *ko-kwai* as 'incense-party', I use the word 'party' in the meaning that it takes in such compounds as 'card-party', 'whist-party', 'chess-party' – for a *ko-kwai* is a meeting held only with the object of playing a game – a very curious game. There are several kinds of incense-games; but in all of them the contest depends upon the ability to remember and to name different kinds of incense by the perfume alone. That variety of *ko-kwai* called *Jitchu-ko* ('ten-burning-incense') is generally conceded to be the most amusing; and I shall try to tell you how it is played.

The numeral 'ten', in the Japanese, or rather Chinese name of this diversion, does not refer to ten kinds, but only to ten packages of incense; for *Jitchu-ko*, besides being the most amusing, is the very simplest of incense-games, and is played with only four kinds of incense. One kind must be supplied by the guests invited to the party; and three are furnished by the person who gives the entertainment. Each of the latter three supplies of incense – usually prepared in packages containing one hundred wafers – is divided into four parts; and each part is put into a separate paper numbered or marked so as to indicate the quality. Thus four packages are prepared of the

1 Girls are still trained in the art of arranging flowers, and in the etiquette of the dainty, though somewhat tedious, *cha-no-yu*. Buddhist priests have long enjoyed a reputation as teachers of the latter. When the pupil has reached a certain degree of proficiency, she is given a diploma or certificate. The tea used in these ceremonies is a powdered tea of remarkable fragrance – the best qualities of which fetch very high prices.

incense classed as No. 1, four of incense No. 2, and four of incense No. 3 – or twelve in all. But the incense given by the guests – always called 'guest-incense' – is not divided: it is only put into a wrapper marked with an abbreviation of the Chinese character signifying 'guest'. Accordingly we have a total of thirteen packages to start with; but three are to be used in the preliminary sampling, or 'experimenting' – as the Japanese term it – after the following manner.

We shall suppose the game to be arranged for a party of six – though there is no rule limiting the number of players. The six take their places in line, or in a half-circle – if the room be small; but they do not sit close together, for reasons which will presently appear. Then the host, or the person appointed to act as incense-burner, prepares a package of the incense classed as No. 1, kindles it in a censer, and passes the censer to the guest occupying the first seat,' [1] with the announcement – 'This is incense No. 1.' The guest receives the censer according to the graceful etiquette required in the *ko-kwai*, inhales the perfume, and passes on the vessel to his neighbour, who receives it in like manner and passes it to the third guest, who presents it to the fourth – and so on. When the censer has gone the round of the party, it is returned to the incense-burner. One package of incense No. 2, and one of No. 3, are similarly prepared, announced, and tested. But with the 'guest-incense' no experiment is made. The player should be able to remember the different odours of the incenses tested; and he is expected to identify the guest-incense at the proper time merely by the unfamiliar quality of its fragrance.

The original thirteen packages having thus by 'experimenting' been reduced to ten, each player is given one set of ten small tablets – usually of gold-lacquer – every set being differently ornamented. The backs only of these tablets are decorated; and the decoration is nearly always a floral design of some sort:– thus one set might be decorated with chrysanthemums in gold, another with tufts of iris-plants, another with a spray of plum-blossoms, etc. But the faces of the tablets bear numbers or marks; and each set comprises three tablets numbered '1', three numbered '2', three numbered '3', and one marked with the character signifying 'guest'. After these tablet-sets have been distributed, a box called the 'tablet-box' is placed before the first player; and all is ready for the real game.

1 The places occupied by guests in a Japanese *zashiki*, or reception room, are numbered from the alcove of the apartment. The place of the most honoured is immediately before the alcove: this is the first seat, and the rest are numbered from it, usually to the left.

The incense-burner retires behind a little screen, shuffles the flat packages like so many cards, takes the uppermost, prepares its contents in the censer, and then, returning to the party, sends the censer upon its round. This time, of course, he does not announce what kind of incense he has used. As the censer passes from hand to hand, each player, after inhaling the fume, puts into the tablet-box one tablet bearing that mark or number which he supposes to be the mark or number of the incense he has smelled. If, for example, he thinks the incense to be 'guest-incense,' he drops into the box that one of his tablets marked with the ideograph meaning 'guest'; or if he believes that he has inhaled the perfume of No. 2, he puts into the box a tablet numbered '2'. When the round is over, tablet-box and censer are both returned to the incense-burner. He takes the six tablets out of the box, and wraps them up in the paper which contained the incense guessed about. The tablets themselves keep the personal as well as the general record – since each player remembers the particular design upon his own set.

The remaining nine packages of incense are consumed and judged in the same way, according to the chance order in which the shuffling has placed them. When all the incense has been used, the tablets are taken out of their wrappings, the record is officially put into writing, and the victor of the day is announced. I here offer the translation of such a record: it will serve to explain, almost at a glance, all the complications of the game.

According to this record the player who used the tablets decorated with the design called 'Young Pine', made but two mistakes; while the holder of the 'White-Lily' set made only one correct guess. But it is quite a feat to make ten correct judgments in succession. The olfactory nerves are apt to become somewhat numbed long before the game is concluded; and, therefore it is customary during the *ko-kwai* to rinse the mouth at intervals with pure vinegar, by which operation the sensitivity is partially restored.

To the Japanese original of the foregoing record were appended the names of the players, the date of the entertainment, and the name of the place where the party was held. It is the custom in some families to enter all such records in a book especially made for the purpose, and furnished with an index which enables the *ko-kwai* player to refer immediately to any interesting fact belonging to the history of any past game.

Names given to the six sets of tablets used, according to the decorative designs on the back:	Order in which the ten packages of incense were used										No. correct
	1 No. 3	2 No. 1	3 G	4 No. 2	5 No. 1	6 No. 3	7 No. 2	8 No. 1	9 No. 3	10 No. 2	
	Guesses recorded by nos. on tablet; correct guesses being marked *										
'Gold Chrysanthemum'	1	3	1	2*	G	1	2*	2	3*	3	3
'Young Bamboo'	3*	1*	2	2*	1*	G	3	2	1	3	4
'Red Peony'	G	1*	2	2*	3	1	3	2	3*	1	3
'White Lily'	1	3	1	3	2	2	1	3	G	2*	1
'Young Pine'	3*	1*	G*	3	1*	2	2*	1*	3*	2*	8
'Cherry-Blossom-in-a-Mist'	1	3	G*	2*	1*	3*	1	2	3*	2*	6

NAMES OF INCENSE USED

1 Tasogare ('Who-Is-there?' i.e. 'Evening-Dusk')
2 Baikwa ('Plum Flower')
3 Wakakusa ('Young Grass')
4 Yamaji-no-Tsuyu ('Dew-on-the-Mountain-Path')
[Guest Incense]

RECORD OF A KO-KWAI

The reader will have noticed that the four kinds of incense used were designated by very pretty names. The incense first mentioned, for example, is called by the poets' name for the gloaming – *tasogare* (lit: 'Who is there?' or 'Who is it?')– a word which in this relation hints of the toilet-perfume that reveals some charming presence to the lover waiting in the dusk. Perhaps some curiosity will be felt regarding the composition of these incenses. I can give the Japanese recipes for two sorts; but I have not been able to identify all of the materials named.

Recipe for *Yamaji-no-Tsuyu* (21 pastilles)

Ingredients	Proportions
Jinko (aloes-wood)	4 *momme* (1/2 oz)
Choji (cloves)	4 *momme* (1/2 oz)
Kunroku (olibanum)	4 *momme* (1/2 oz)
Hakko (artemisia Schmidtiana)	4 *momme* (1/2 oz)
Jako (musk)	1 *bu* (1/8 oz)
Koko (?)	4 *momme* (1/2 oz)

Recipe for *Baikwa* (50 pastilles)

Ingredients	Proportions
Jinko (aloes)	20 *momme* (2 1/2 oz)
Choji (cloves)	12 *momme* (1 1/2 oz)
Koko (?)	8 1/3 *momme* (1 1/40 oz)
Byakudan (sandalwood)	4 *momme* (1/2 oz)
Kansho (spikenard)	2 *bu* (1/4 oz)
Kwakko (Bishop's-wort?)	1 *bu* 2 *sbu* (3/16 oz)
Kunroku (olibanum)	3 *bu* 3 *sbu* (15/22 oz)
Shomokko (?)	2 *bu* (1/4 oz)
Jako (musk)	3 *bu* 2 *sbu* (7/16 oz)
Ryuno (refined Borneo Camphor)	3 *sbu* (3/8 oz)

The incense used at a *ko-kwai* ranges in value, according to the style of the entertainment, from $2.50 to $30.00 per envelope of 100 wafers – wafers usually not more than one-fourth of an inch in diameter. Sometimes an incense is used worth even more than $30.00 per envelope: this contains *ranjatai*, an aromatic of which the perfume is compared to that of 'musk mingled with orchid-flowers'. But there is some incense – never sold – which is much more precious than *ranjatai* – incense valued less for its composition than for its history: I mean the incense brought centuries ago from China or from India by the Buddhist missionaries, and presented to princes or to other persons of high rank. Several ancient Japanese temples also include such foreign incense among their treasures. And very rarely a little of this priceless material is contributed to an incense-party – much as in Europe, on very extraordinary occasions, some banquet is glorified by the production of a wine several hundred years old.

Like the tea-ceremonies, the *ko-kwai* exact observance of a very complex and ancient etiquette. But this subject could interest few readers; and I shall only mention some of the rules regarding preparations and precautions. First of all, it is required that the person invited to an incense-party shall attend the same in as *odourless* a condition as possible: a lady, for instance, must not use hair-oil, or put on any dress that has been kept in a perfumed chest-of-drawers. Furthermore, the guest should prepare for the contest by taking a prolonged hot bath, and should eat only the lightest and least odorous kind of food before going to the rendezvous. It is forbidden to leave the room during the game, or to open any door or window, or to indulge in needless conversation. Finally I may observe that, while judging the incense, a player is expected to take not less than three inhalations, or more than five.

In this economical era, the *ko-kwai* takes of necessity a much humbler form than it assumed in the time of the great daimyo, of the princely abbots, and of the military aristocracy. A full set of the utensils required for the game can now be had for about $50.00; but the materials are of the poorest kind. The old-fashioned sets were fantastically expensive. Some were worth thousands of dollars. The incense-burner's desk (the writing-box, paper-box, tablet-box, etc.), the various stands or *dai* – were of the costliest gold-lacquer; the pincers and other instruments were of gold, curiously worked; and the censer – whether of precious metal, bronze, or porcelain – was always a *chef-d'oeuvre*, designed by some artist of renown.

5

Although the original signification of incense in Buddhist ceremonies was chiefly symbolical, there is good reason to suppose that various beliefs older than Buddhism – some, perhaps, peculiar to the race, others probably of Chinese or Korean derivation – began at an early period to influence the popular use of incense in Japan. Incense is still burned in the presence of a corpse with the idea that its fragrance shields both corpse and newly-parted soul from malevolent demons; and by the peasants it is often burned also to drive away goblins and the evil powers presiding over diseases. But formerly it was used to summon spirits as well as to banish them. Allusions to its employment in various weird rites may be found in some of the old dramas and romances. One particular sort of incense, imported from China, was said to have the power of calling up human spirits. This was the wizard-incense referred to in such ancient love-songs as the following:

> *I have heard of the magical incense that summons the souls of the absent:*
> *Would I had some to burn, in the nights when I wait alone!*

There is an interesting mention of this incense in the Chinese book, *Shang-hai-king*. It was called *Fwan-hwan-hiang* (by Japanese pronunciation, *Hangon-ko*), or 'Spirit-Recalling-Incense'; and it was made in Tso-Chau, or the District of the Ancestors, situated by the Eastern Sea. To summon the ghost of any dead person – or even that of a living person, according to some authorities – it was only necessary to kindle some of the incense, and to pronounce certain words, while keeping the mind fixed upon the memory of that person. Then, in the smoke of the incense, the remembered face and form would appear.

In many old Japanese and Chinese books mention is made of a famous story about this incense – a story of the Chinese Emperor Wu, of the Han dynasty. When the Emperor had lost his beautiful favourite, the Lady Li, he sorrowed so much that fears were entertained for his reason. But all efforts made to divert his mind from the thought of her proved unavailing. One day he ordered some Spirit-Recalling-Incense to be procured, that he might summon her from the dead. His counsellors prayed him to forego his purpose, declaring that the vision could only intensify his grief. But he gave no heed to their advice, and himself performed the rite – kindling the incense, and keeping his mind fixed upon the memory of the Lady Li. Presently, within the thick blue smoke arising from the incense, the outline of a feminine form became visible. It defined, took tints of life, slowly became luminous, and the Emperor recognised the form of his beloved At first the apparition was faint; but it soon became distinct as a living person, and seemed with each moment to grow more beautiful. The Emperor whispered to the vision, but received no answer. He called aloud, and the presence made no sign. Then, unable to control himself, he approached the censer. But the instant that he touched the smoke, the phantom trembled and vanished.

Japanese artists are still occasionally inspired by the legends of the *Hangon-ko*. Only last year, in Tokyo, at an exhibition of new *kake-mono*, I saw a picture of a young wife kneeling before an alcove wherein the smoke of the magical incense was shaping the shadow of the absent husband.[1]

Although the power of making visible the forms of the dead has been claimed for one sort of incense only, the burning of any kind of incense is supposed to summon viewless spirits in multitude. These come to devour the smoke. They are called *Jiki-ko-ki*, or 'incense-eating goblins;' and they belong to the fourteenth of the thirty-six classes of Gaki (*pretas*) recognised by Japanese Buddhism. They are the ghosts of men who anciently, for the sake of gain, made or sold bad incense; and by the evil karma of that action they now find themselves in the state of hunger-suffering spirits, and compelled to seek their only food in the smoke of incense.

[1] Among the curious Tokyo inventions of 1898 was a new variety of cigarettes called *Hangon-so*, or 'Herb of Hangon' – a name suggesting that their smoke operated like the spirit-summoning incense. As a matter of fact, the chemical action of the tobacco-smoke would define, upon a paper fitted into the mouth-piece of each cigarette, the photographic image of a dancing-girl.

A STORY OF DIVINATION

A Story of Divination

I once knew a fortune-teller who really believed in the science that he professed. He had learned, as a student of the old Chinese philosophy, to believe in divination long before he thought of practising it. During his youth he had been in the service of a wealthy daimyo, but subsequently, like thousands of other samurai, found himself reduced to desperate straits by the social and political changes of Meiji. It was then that he became a fortune-teller – an itinerant *uranaiya* – travelling on foot from town to town, and returning to his home rarely more than once a year with the proceeds of his journey. As a fortune-teller he was tolerably successful – chiefly, I think, because of his perfect sincerity, and because of a peculiar gentle manner that invited confidence. His system was the old scholarly one: he used the book known to English readers as the *Yi-King* – also a set of ebony blocks which could be so arranged as to form any of the Chinese hexagrams – and he always began his divination with an earnest prayer to the gods.

The system itself he held to be infallible in the hands of a master. He confessed that he had made some erroneous predictions; but he said that these mistakes had been entirely due to his own miscomprehension of certain texts or diagrams. To do him justice I must mention that in my own case – he told my fortune four times – his predictions were fulfilled in such wise that I became afraid of them. You may disbelieve in fortune-telling – intellectually scorn it – but something of inherited superstitious tendency lurks within most of us; and a few strange experiences can so appeal to that inheritance as to induce the most unreasoning hope or fear of the good or bad luck promised you by some diviner. Really to see our future would be a misery. Imagine the result of knowing that there must happen to you, within the next two months, some terrible misfortune which you cannot possibly provide against!

He was already an old man when I first saw him in Izumo – certainly more than sixty years of age, but looking very much younger. Afterwards I met him in Osaka, in Kyoto, and in Kobe. More than once I tried to persuade him to pass the colder months of the winter-season under my roof – for he possessed an extraordinary knowledge of traditions, and could have been of inestimable service to me in a literary way. But partly because the habit of wandering had become with him a second nature, and partly because of a love of independence as savage as a gypsy's, I was never able to keep him with me for more than two days at a time.

Every year he used to come to Tokyo – usually in the latter part of autumn. Then, for several weeks, he would flit about the city, from district to district, and vanish again. But during these fugitive trips he never failed to visit me, bringing welcome news of Izumo people and places – bringing also some queer little present, generally of a religious kind, from some famous place of pilgrimage. On these occasions I could get a few hours' chat with him. Sometimes the talk was of strange things seen or heard during his recent journey; sometimes it turned upon old legends or beliefs; sometimes it was about fortune-telling. The last time we met he told me of an exact Chinese science of divination which he regretted never having been able to learn.

'Anyone learned in that science,' he said, 'would be able, for example, not only to tell you the exact time at which any post or beam of this house will yield to decay, but even to tell you the direction of the breaking, and all its results. I can best explain what I mean by relating a story.

'The story is about the famous Chinese fortune-teller whom we call in Japan Shoko Setsu, and it is written in the book *Baikwa-Shin-Eki*, which is a book of divination. While still a very young man, Shoko Setsu obtained a high position by reason of his learning and virtue; but he resigned it and went into solitude that he might give his whole time to study. For years thereafter he lived alone in a hut among the mountains; studying without a fire in winter, and without a fan in summer; writing his thoughts upon the wall of his room – for lack of paper – and using only a tile for his pillow.

'One day, in the period of greatest summer heat, he found himself overcome by drowsiness; and he lay down to rest, with his tile under his head. Scarcely had he fallen asleep when a rat ran across his face and woke him with a start. Feeling angry, he seized his tile and flung it at the rat; but the rat escaped unhurt, and the tile was broken. Shoko Setsu looked sorrowfully at the fragments of his pillow, and reproached himself for his hastiness. Then suddenly he perceived, upon the freshly exposed clay of the broken tile, some Chinese characters – between the upper and lower surfaces. Thinking this very strange, he picked up the pieces, and carefully examined them. He found that along the line of fracture seventeen characters had been written within the clay before the tile had been baked; and the characters read thus: "In the Year of the Hare, in the fourth month, on the seventeenth day, at the Hour of the Serpent, this tile, after serving as a pillow, will be thrown at a rat and broken." Now the prediction had really been fulfilled at the Hour of the Serpent on the seventeenth day of the fourth month of the Year of the Hare. Greatly astonished, Shoko Setsu once again looked at the fragments, and discovered the seal and the name of the maker. At once he left his hut, and, taking with him the pieces of the tile, hurried to the neighbouring town in search of the tile-maker. He found the tile-maker in the course of the day, showed him the broken tile, and asked him about its history.

'After having carefully examined the shards, the tile-maker said: "This tile was made in my house; but the characters in the clay were written by an old man – a fortune-teller – who asked permission to write upon the tile before it was baked." "Do you know where he lives?" asked Shoko Setsu. "He used to live," the tile-maker answered, "not very far from here; and I can show you the way to the house. But I do not know his name."

'Having been guided to the house, Shoko Setsu presented himself at the entrance, and asked for permission to speak to the old man. A serving-student courteously invited him to enter, and ushered him into an apartment where several young men were at study. As Shoko Setsu took his seat, all the youths saluted him. Then the one who had first addressed him bowed and said: "We are grieved to inform you that our master died a few days ago. But we have been waiting for you, because he predicted that you would come today to this house, at this very hour. Your name is Shoko Setsu. And our master told us to give you a book which he believed would be of service to you. Here is the book – please to accept it."

'Shoko Setsu was not less delighted than surprised; for the book was a manuscript of the rarest and most precious kind – containing all the secrets of the science of divination. After having thanked the young men, and properly expressed his regret for the death of their teacher, he went back to his hut, and there immediately proceeded to test the worth of the book by consulting its pages in regard to his own fortune. The book suggested to him that on the south side of his dwelling, at a particular spot near one corner of the hut, great luck awaited him. He dug at the place indicated, and found a jar containing gold enough to make him a very wealthy man.'

*   *   *

My old acquaintance left this world as lonesomely as he had lived in it. Last winter, while crossing a mountain-range, he was overtaken by a snowstorm, and lost his way. Many days later he was found standing erect at the foot of a pine, with his little pack strapped to his shoulders: a statue of ice – arms folded and eyes closed as in meditation. Probably, while waiting for the storm to pass, he had yielded to the drowsiness of cold, and the drift had risen over him as he slept. Hearing of this strange death I remembered the old Japanese saying – *uranaiya minouye shiradzu*: 'The fortune-teller knows not his own fate.'

SILKWORMS

Silkworms

I

I was puzzled by the phrase, 'silkworm-moth eyebrow', in an old Japanese, or rather Chinese, proverb – *The silkworm-moth eyebrow of a woman is the axe that cuts down the wisdom of man.* So I went to my friend Niimi, who keeps silkworms, to ask for an explanation.

'Is it possible,' he exclaimed, 'that you never saw a silkworm-moth? The silkworm-moth has very beautiful eyebrows.'

'Eyebrows?' I queried, in astonishment. 'Well, call them what you like,' returned Niimi – 'the poets call them eyebrows . . . Wait a moment, and I will show you.'

He left the guest-room, and presently returned with a white paper-fan, on which a silkworm-moth was sleepily reposing.

'We always reserve a few for breeding,' he said – 'this one is just out of the cocoon. It cannot fly, of course: none of them can fly . . . Now look at the eyebrows.'

I looked, and saw that the antennae, very short and feathery, were so arched back over the two jewel-specks of eyes in the velvety head, as to give the appearance of a really handsome pair of eyebrows.

Then Niimi took me to see his worms.

In Niimi's neighbourhood, where there are plenty of mulberry trees, many families keep silkworms – the tending and feeding being mostly done by women and children. The worms are kept in large oblong trays, elevated upon light wooden stands about three feet high. It is curious to see hundreds of caterpillars feeding all together in one tray, and to hear the soft papery noise which they make while gnawing their mulberry-leaves. As they approach maturity, the creatures need almost constant attention. At brief intervals some expert visits each tray to inspect progress, picks up the plumpest feeders, and decides, by gently rolling them between forefinger and thumb, which are ready to spin. These are dropped into covered boxes, where they soon swathe themselves out of sight in white floss. A few only of the best are suffered to emerge from their silky sleep – the selected breeders. They have beautiful wings, but cannot use them. They have mouths, but do not eat. They only pair, lay eggs, and die. For thousands of years their race has been so well cared for, that it can no longer take any care of itself.

It was the evolutional lesson of this latter fact that chiefly occupied me while Niimi and his younger brother (who feeds the worms) were kindly explaining the methods of the industry. They told me curious things about different breeds, and also about a wild variety of silkworm that cannot be domesticated – it spins splendid silk before turning into a vigorous moth which can use its wings to some purpose. But I fear that I did not act like a person who felt interested in the subject; for, even while I tried to listen, I began to muse.

2

First of all, I found myself thinking about a delightful reverie by M. Anatole France, in which he says that if he had been the Demiurge, he would have put youth at the end of life instead of at the beginning, and would have otherwise so ordered matters that every human being should have three stages of development, somewhat corresponding to those of the lepidoptera. Then it occurred to me that this fantasy was in substance scarcely more than the delicate modification of a most ancient doctrine, common to nearly all the higher forms of religion.

Western faiths especially teach that our life on earth is a larval state of greedy helplessness, and that death is a pupa-sleep out of which we should soar into everlasting light. They tell us that during its sentient existence, the outer body should be thought of only as a kind of caterpillar, and thereafter as a chrysalis – and they aver that we lose or gain, according to our behaviour as larvae, the power to develop wings under the mortal wrapping. Also they tell us not to trouble ourselves about the fact that we see no Psyche-imago detach itself from the broken cocoon: this lack of visual evidence signifies nothing, because we have only the purblind vision of grubs. Our eyes are but half-evolved. Do not whole scales of colours invisibly exist above and below the limits of our retinal sensibility? Even so the butterfly-man exists – although, as a matter of course, we cannot see him.

But what would become of this human imago in a state of perfect bliss? From the evolutional point of view the question has interest; and its obvious answer was suggested to me by the history of those silkworms – which have been domesticated for only a few thousand years. Consider the result of our celestial domestication for – let us say – several millions of years: I mean the final consequence, to the wishers, of being able to gratify every wish at will.

Those silkworms have all that they wish for – even considerably more. Their wants, though very simple, are fundamentally identical with the necessities of mankind – food, shelter, warmth, safety, and comfort. Our endless social struggle is mainly for these things. Our dream of heaven is the dream of obtaining them free of cost in pain; and the condition of those silkworms is the realisation, in a small way, of our imagined Paradise. (I am not considering the fact that a vast majority of the worms are predestined to torment and the second death; for my theme is of heaven, not of lost souls. I am speaking of the elect – those worms preordained to salvation and rebirth.) Probably they can feel only very weak sensations: they are certainly incapable of prayer. But if they were able to pray, they could not ask for anything more than they already receive from the youth who feeds and tends them. He is their providence – a god of whose existence they can be aware in only the vaguest possible way, but just such a god as they require. And we should foolishly deem ourselves fortunate to be equally well cared-for in proportion to our more complex wants. Do not our common forms of prayer prove our desire for like attention? Is not the assertion of our 'need of divine love' an involuntary confession that we wish to be treated like silkworms – to live without pain by the help of gods? Yet if the gods were to treat us as we want, we should presently afford fresh evidence – in the way of what is called 'the evidence from degeneration' – that the great evolutional law is far above the gods.

An early stage of that degeneration would be represented by total incapacity to help ourselves – then we should begin to lose the use of our higher sense-organs – later on, the brain would shrink to a vanishing pinpoint of matter – still later we should dwindle into mere amorphous sacs, mere blind stomachs. Such would be the physical consequence of that kind of divine love which we so lazily wish for. The longing for perpetual bliss in perpetual peace might well seem a malevolent inspiration from the Lords of Death and

Darkness. All life that feels and thinks has been, and can continue to be, only as the product of struggle and pain – only as the outcome of endless battle with the Powers of the Universe. And cosmic law is uncompromising. Whatever organ ceases to know pain – whatever faculty ceases to be used under the stimulus of pain – must also cease to exist. Let pain and its effort be suspended, and life must shrink back, first into protoplasmic shapelessness, thereafter into dust.

Buddhism – which, in its own grand way, is a doctrine of evolution – rationally proclaims its heaven but a higher stage of development through pain, and teaches that even in paradise the cessation of effort produces degradation. With equal reasonableness it declares that the capacity for pain in the superhuman world increases always in proportion to the capacity for pleasure. (There is little fault to be found with this teaching from a scientific standpoint – since we know that higher evolution must involve an increase of sensitivity to pain.) In the Heavens of Desire, says the *Shobo-nen-jo-kyo*, the pain of death is so great that all the agonies of all the hells united could equal but one-sixteenth part of such pain.[1]

The foregoing comparison is unnecessarily strong; but the Buddhist teaching about heaven is in substance eminently logical. The suppression of pain – mental or physical – in any conceivable state of sentient existence, would necessarily involve the suppression also of pleasure – and certainly all progress, whether moral or material, depends upon the power to meet and to master pain. In a silkworm-paradise such as our mundane instincts lead us to desire, the seraph freed from the necessity of toil, and able to satisfy his every want at will, would lose his wings at last, and sink back to the condition of a grub . . .

3

I told the substance of my reverie to Niimi. He used to be a great reader of Buddhist books.

'Well,' he said, 'I was reminded of a queer Buddhist story by the proverb that you asked me to explain – *The silkworm-moth eyebrow of a woman is the axe that cuts down the wisdom of man*. According to

1 This statement refers only to the Heavens of Sensuous Pleasure – not to the Paradise of Amida, nor to those heavens into which one enters by the Apparitional Birth. But even in the highest and most immaterial zones of being – in the Heavens of Formlessness – the cessation of effort and of the pain of effort involves the penalty of rebirth in a lower state of existence.

our doctrine, the saying would be as true of life in heaven as of life upon earth . . . This is the story: 'When Shaka[1] dwelt in this world, one of his disciples, called Nanda, was bewitched by the beauty of a woman; and Shaka desired to save him from the results of this illusion. So he took Nanda to a wild place in the mountains where there were apes, and showed him a very ugly female ape, and asked him: "Which is the more beautiful, Nanda – the woman that you love, or this female ape?" "Oh, Master!" exclaimed Nanda, "how can a lovely woman be compared with an ugly ape?" "Perhaps you will presently find reason to make the comparison yourself," answered the Buddha – and instantly by supernatural power he ascended with Nanda to the *San-jusan-Ten*, which is the Second of the Six Heavens of Desire. There, within a palace of jewels, Nanda saw a multitude of heavenly maidens celebrating some festival with music and dance; and the beauty of the least among them incomparably exceeded that of the fairest woman of earth. "O Master," cried Nanda, "what wonderful festival is this?" "Ask some of those people," responded Shaka. So Nanda questioned one of the celestial maidens; and she said to him: "This festival is to celebrate the good tidings that have been brought to us. There is now in the human world, among the disciples of Shaka, a most excellent youth called Nanda, who is soon to be reborn into this heaven, and to become our bridegroom, because of his holy life. We wait for him with rejoicing." This reply filled the heart of Nanda with delight. Then the Buddha asked him: "Is there any one among these maidens, Nanda, equal in beauty to the woman with whom you have been in love?" "Nay, Master!" answered Nanda; "even as that woman surpassed in beauty the female ape that we saw on the mountain, so is she herself surpassed by even the least among these."

'Then the Buddha immediately descended with Nanda to the depths of the hells, and took him into a torture-chamber where myriads of men and women were being boiled alive in great cauldrons, and otherwise horribly tormented by devils. Then Nanda found himself standing before a huge vessel which was filled with molten metal – and he feared and wondered because this vessel had as yet no occupant. An idle devil sat beside it, yawning. "Master," Nanda inquired of the Buddha, "for whom has this vessel been prepared?" "Ask the devil," answered Shaka. Nanda did so; and the devil said to him: "There is a man called Nanda – now one of

1 Sakyamuni.

Shaka's disciples – about to be reborn into one of the heavens, on account of his former good actions. But after having there indulged himself, he is to be reborn in this hell; and his place will be in that pot. I am waiting for him." ' [1]

1 I give the story substantially as it was told to me; but I have not been able to compare it with any published text. My friend says that he has seen two Chinese versions – one in the *Hongyo-kyo* (?), the other in the *Zoichi-agon-kyo* (Ekottaragamas). In Mr Henry Clarke Warren's *Buddhism in Translations* (the most interesting and valuable single volume of its kind that I have ever seen), there is a Pali version of the legend, which differs considerably from the above – this Nanda, according to Mr. Warren's work, was a prince, and the younger half-brother of Sakyamuni.

A PASSIONAL KARMA

A Passional Karma

One of the never-failing attractions of the Tokyo stage is the performance, by the famous Kikugoro and his company, of the *Botan-
Doro*, or 'Peony-Lantern'. This weird play, of which the scenes
are laid in the middle of the last century, is the dramatisation of
a romance by the novelist Encho, written in colloquial Japanese, and
purely Japanese in local colour, though inspired by a Chinese tale.
I went to see the play; and Kikugoro made me familiar with a new
variety of the pleasure of fear. 'Why not give English readers the
ghostly part of the story?' – asked a friend who guides me betimes
through the mazes of Eastern philosophy. 'It would serve to explain
some popular ideas of the supernatural which Western people know
very little about. And I could help you with the translation.'

I gladly accepted the suggestion; and we composed the following
summary of the more extraordinary portion of Encho's romance.
Here and there we found it necessary to condense the original narrative; and we tried to keep close to the text only in the conversational
passages – some of which happen to possess a particular quality of
psychological interest.

* * *

*This is the story of the Ghosts in the Romance
of the Peony-Lantern.*

I

There once lived in the district of Ushigome, in Yedo, a *hatamoto* [1]
called Iijima Heizayemon, whose only daughter, Tsuyu, was beautiful as her name, which signifies 'Morning Dew'. Iijima took a second
wife when his daughter was about sixteen; and, finding that O-Tsuyu

[1] The *hatamoto* were samurai forming the special military force of the Shogun.
The name literally signifies 'Banner-Supporters'. These were the highest class
of samurai – not only as the immediate vassals of the Shogun, but as a military
aristocracy.

could not be happy with her mother-in-law, he had a pretty villa built for the girl at Yanagijima, as a separate residence, and gave her an excellent maidservant, called O-Yone, to wait upon her.

O-Tsuyu lived happily enough in her new home until one day when the family physician, Yamamoto Shijo, paid her a visit in company with a young samurai named Hagiwara Shinzaburo, who resided in the Nedzu quarter. Shinzaburo was an unusually handsome lad, and very gentle; and the two young people fell in love with each other at sight. Even before the brief visit was over, they contrived – unheard by the old doctor – to pledge themselves to each other for life. And, at parting, O-Tsuyu whispered to the youth – '*Remember! If you do not come to see me again, I shall certainly die!*'

Shinzaburo never forgot those words; and he was only too eager to see more of O-Tsuyu. But etiquette forbade him to make the visit alone: he was obliged to wait for some other chance to accompany the doctor, who had promised to take him to the villa a second time. Unfortunately the old man did not keep this promise. He had perceived the sudden affection of O-Tsuyu; and he feared that her father would hold him responsible for any serious results. Iijima Heizayemon had a reputation for cutting off heads. And the more Shijo thought about the possible consequences of his introduction of Shinzaburo at the Iijima villa, the more he became afraid. Therefore he purposely abstained from calling upon his young friend.

Months passed; and O-Tsuyu, little imagining the true cause of Shinzaburo's neglect, believed that her love had been scorned. Then she pined away, and died. Soon afterwards, the faithful servant O-Yone also died, through grief at the loss of her mistress; and the two were buried side by side in the cemetery of Shin-Banzui-In – a temple which still stands in the neighbourhood of Dango-Zaka, where the famous chrysanthemum-shows are yearly held.

2

Shinzaburo knew nothing of what had happened; but his disappointment and his anxiety had resulted in a prolonged illness. He was slowly recovering, but still very weak, when he unexpectedly received another visit from Yamamoto Shijo. The old man made a number of plausible excuses for his apparent neglect. Shinzaburo said to him: 'I have been sick ever since the beginning of spring –

even now I cannot eat anything . . . Was it not rather unkind of you never to call? I thought that we were to make another visit together to the house of the Lady Iijima; and I wanted to take to her some little present as a return for our kind reception. Of course I could not go by myself.'

Shijo gravely responded – 'I am very sorry to tell you that the young lady is dead!'

'Dead!' repeated Shinzaburo, turning white – 'did you say that she is dead?'

The doctor remained silent for a moment, as if collecting himself; then he resumed, in the quick light tone of a man resolved not to take trouble seriously: 'My great mistake was in having introduced you to her; for it seems that she fell in love with you at once. I am afraid that you must have said something to encourage this affection – when you were in that little room together. At all events, I saw how she felt towards you; and then I became uneasy – fearing that her father might come to hear of the matter, and lay the whole blame upon me. So – to be quite frank with you – I decided that it would be better not to call upon you; and I purposely stayed away for a long time. But, only a few days ago, happening to visit Iijima's house, I heard, to my great surprise, that his daughter had died, and that her servant O-Yone had also died. Then, remembering all that had taken place, I knew that the young lady must have died of love for you . . . [*laughing*] Ah, you are really a sinful fellow! Yes, you are! [*laughing*] Isn't it a sin to have been born so handsome that the girls die for love of you?¹ [*seriously*] Well, we must leave the dead to the dead. It is no use to talk further about the matter – all that you now can do for her is to repeat the Nembutsu² . . . Good-bye.'

And the old man retired hastily – anxious to avoid further converse about the painful event for which he felt himself to have been un-wittingly responsible.

3

Shinzaburo long remained stupefied with grief by the news of O-Tsuyu's death. But as soon as he found himself again able to think clearly, he inscribed the dead girl's name upon a mortuary tablet, and placed the tablet in the Buddhist shrine of his house, and set

1 Perhaps this conversation may seem strange to the Western reader; but it is true to life. The whole of the scene is characteristically Japanese.
2 The invocation *Namu Amida Butsu*! ('Hail to the Buddha Amitabha!') repeated, as a prayer, for the sake of the dead.

offerings before it, and recited prayers. Every day thereafter he presented offerings, and repeated the Nembutsu; and the memory of O-Tsuyu was never absent from his thought.

Nothing occurred to change the monotony of his solitude before the time of the Bon – the great Festival of the Dead – which begins upon the thirteenth day of the seventh month. Then he decorated his house, and prepared everything for the festival – hanging out the lanterns that guide the returning spirits, and setting the food of ghosts on the *shoryodana*, or Shelf of Souls. And on the first evening of the Ban, after sundown, he kindled a small lamp before the tablet of O-Tsuyu, and lighted the lanterns.

The night was clear, with a great moon – and windless, and very warm. Shinzaburo sought the coolness of his veranda. Clad only in a light summer-robe, he sat there thinking, dreaming, sorrowing – sometimes fanning himself, sometimes making a little smoke to drive the mosquitoes away. Everything was quiet. It was a lonesome neighbourhood, and there were few passers-by. He could hear only the soft rushing of a neighbouring stream, and the shrilling of night-insects.

But all at once this stillness was broken by a sound of women's *geta* [1] approaching – *kara-kon, kara-kon* – and the sound drew nearer and nearer, quickly, till it reached the live-hedge surrounding the garden. Then Shinzaburoe, feeling curious, stood on tiptoe, so as to look Over the hedge; and he saw two women passing. One, who was carrying a beautiful lantern decorated with peony-flowers, [2] appeared to be a servant – the other was a slender girl of about seventeen, wearing a long-sleeved robe embroidered with designs of autumn-blossoms. Almost at the same instant both women turned their faces toward Shinzaburo – and to his utter astonishment, he recognised O-Tsuyu and her servant O-Yone.

They stopped immediately; and the girl cried out: 'Oh, how strange! . . . Hagiwara Sama!'

Shinzaburo simultaneously called to the maid: 'O-Yone! Ah, you are O-Yone! – I remember you very well.'

---

1 *Komageta* in the original. The *geta* is a wooden sandal, or clog, of which there are many varieties – some decidedly elegant. The *komageta*, or 'pony-*geta*' is so-called because of the sonorous hoof-like echo which it makes on hard ground.

2 The sort of lantern here referred to is no longer made; it was totally unlike the modern domestic band-lantern, painted with the owner's crest; but it was not altogether unlike some forms of lanterns still manufactured for the Festival of the Dead, and called *Bon-doro*. The flowers ornamenting it were not painted: they were artificial flowers of crepe-silk, and were attached to the top of the lantern.

'Hagiwara Sama!' exclaimed O-Yone in a tone of supreme amazement. 'Never could I have believed it possible! . . . Sir, we were told that you had died.'

'How extraordinary!' cried Shinzaburo. 'Why, I was told that both of you were dead!'

'Ah, what a hateful story!' returned O-Yone. 'Why repeat such unlucky words? . . . Who told you?'

'Please to come in,' said Shinzaburo – 'here we can talk better. The garden-gate is open.'

So they entered, and exchanged greeting; and when Shinzaburo had made them comfortable, he said: 'I trust that you will pardon my discourtesy in not having called upon you for so long a time. But Shijo, the doctor, about a month ago, told me that you had both died.'

'So it was he who told you?' exclaimed O-Yone. 'It was very wicked of him to say such a thing. Well, it was also Shijo who told us that you were dead. I think that he wanted to deceive you – which was not a difficult thing to do, because you are so confiding and trustful. Possibly my mistress betrayed her liking for you in some words which found their way to her father's ears; and, in that case, O-Kuni – the new wife – might have planned to make the doctor tell you that we were dead, so as to bring about a separation. Anyhow, when my mistress heard that you had died, she wanted to cut off her hair immediately, and to become a nun. But I was able to prevent her from cutting off her hair; and I persuaded her at last to become a nun only in her heart. Afterwards her father wished her to marry a certain young man; and she refused. Then there was a great deal of trouble – chiefly caused by O-Kuni – and we went away from the villa, and found a very small house in Yanaka-no-Sasaki. There we are now just barely able to live, by doing a little private work . . . My mistress has been constantly repeating the *Nembutsu* for your sake. Today, being the first day of the Bon, we went to visit the temples; and we were on our way home – thus late – when this strange meeting happened.'

'Oh, how extraordinary!' cried Shinzaburo. 'Can it be true? Or is it only a dream? Here I, too, have been constantly reciting the *Nembutsu* before a tablet with her name upon it! Look!' And he showed them O-Tsuyu's tablet in its place upon the Shelf of Souls.

'We are more than grateful for your kind remembrance,' returned O-Yone, smiling . . . 'Now as for my mistress,' she continued, turning towards O-Tsuyu, who had all the while remained demure and silent, half-hiding her face with her sleeve – 'as for my mistress, she actually says that she would not mind being disowned by her father for the time of seven existences,[1] or even being killed by him, for your sake! Come! Will you not allow her to stay here tonight?'

Shinzaburo turned pale for joy. He answered in a voice trembling with emotion: 'Please remain; but do not speak loud – because there is a troublesome fellow living close by – a *ninsomi*[2] called Hakuodo Yusai, who tells people's fortunes by looking at their faces. He is inclined to be curious; and it is better that he should not know.'

The two women remained that night in the house of the young samurai, and returned to their own home a little before daybreak. And after that night they came every night for seven nights – whether the weather were foul or fair – always at the same hour. And Shinzaburo became more and more attached to the girl; and the twain were fettered, each to each, by that bond of illusion which is stronger than bands of iron.

4

Now there was a man called Tomozo, who lived in a small cottage adjoining Shinzaburo's residence. Tomozo and his wife O-Mine were both employed by Shinzaburo as servants. Both seemed to be devoted to their young master; and by his help they were able to live in comparative comfort.

One night, at a very late hour, Tomozo heard the voice of a woman in his master's apartment; and this made him uneasy. He feared that Shinzaburo, being very gentle and affectionate, might be made the dupe of some cunning wanton – in which event the domestics would be the first to suffer. He therefore resolved to watch; and on the following night he stole on tiptoe to Shinzaburo's dwelling, and looked through a chink in one of the sliding shutters. By the glow of a night-lantern within the sleeping-room, he was able to perceive that his master and a strange woman were

1 'For the time of seven existences' – that is to say, for the time of seven successive lives. In Japanese drama and romance it is not uncommon to represent a father as disowning his child 'for the time of seven lives'. Such a disowning is called *shichi-sho made no mando*, a disinheritance for seven lives – signifying that in six future lives after the present the erring son or daughter will continue to feel the parental displeasure.

2 The profession is not yet extinct. The *ninsomi* uses a kind of magnifying glass (or magnifying-mirror sometimes), called *tengankyo* or *ninsomegane*.

talking together under the mosquito-net. At first he could not see the woman distinctly. Her back was turned to him – he only observed that she was very slim, and that she appeared to be very young – judging from the fashion of her dress and hair.[1] Putting his ear to the chink, he could hear the conversation plainly. The woman said: 'And if I should be disowned by my father, would you then let me come and live with you?'

Shinzaburo answered: 'Most assuredly I would – nay, I should be glad of the chance. But there is no reason to fear that you will ever be disowned by your father; for you are his only daughter, and he loves you very much. What I do fear is that some day we shall be cruelly separated.'

She responded softly: 'Never, never could I even think of accepting any other man for my husband. Even if our secret were to become known, and my father were to kill me for what I have done, still – after death itself – I could never cease to think of you. And I am now quite sure that you yourself would not be able to live very long without me . . . ' Then clinging closely to him, with her lips at his neck, she caressed him; and he returned her caresses.

Tomozo wondered as he listened – because the language of the woman was not the language of a common woman, but the language of a lady of rank.[2] Then he determined at all hazards to get one glimpse of her face; and he crept round the house, backwards and forwards, peering through every crack and chink. And at last he was able to see – but therewith an icy trembling seized him; and the hair of his head stood up.

For the face was the face of a woman long dead – and the fingers caressing were fingers of naked bone – and of the body below the waist there was not anything: it melted off into thinnest trailing shadow. Where the eyes of the lover deluded saw youth and grace and beauty, there appeared to the eyes of the watcher horror only, and the emptiness of death. Simultaneously another woman's figure, and a weirder, rose up from within the chamber, and swiftly made toward the watcher, as if discerning his presence. Then, in uttermost terror, he fled to the dwelling of Hakuodo Yusai, and, knocking frantically at the doors, succeeded in arousing him.

---

1 The colour and form of the dress, and the style of wearing the hair, are by Japanese custom regulated according to the age of the woman.
2 The forms of speech used by the samurai, and other superior classes, differed considerably from those of the popular idiom; but these differences could not be effectively rendered into English.

5

Hakuodo Yusai, the *ninsomi*, was a very old man; but in his time he had travelled much, and he had heard and seen so many things that he could not be easily surprised. Yet the story of the terrified Tomozo both alarmed and amazed him. He had read in ancient Chinese books of love between the living and the dead; but he had never believed it possible. Now, however, he felt convinced that the statement of Tomozo was not a falsehood, and that something very strange was really going on in the house of Hagiwara. Should the truth prove to be what Tomozo imagined, then the young samurai was a doomed man.

'If the woman be a ghost' – said Yusai to the frightened servant, ' – if the woman be a ghost, your master must die very soon – unless something extraordinary can be done to save him. And if the woman be a ghost, the signs of death will appear upon his face. For the spirit of the living is *yoki*, and pure – the spirit of the dead is *inki*, and unclean: the one is Positive, the other Negative. He whose bride is a ghost cannot live. Even though in his blood there existed the force of a life of one hundred years, that force must quickly perish . . . Still, I shall do all that I can to save Hagiwara Sama. And in the meantime, Tomozo, say nothing to any other person – not even to your wife – about this matter. At sunrise I shall call upon your master.'

6

When questioned next morning by Yusai, Shinzaburo at first attempted to deny that any women had been visiting the house; but finding this artless policy of no avail, and perceiving that the old man's purpose was altogether unselfish, he was finally persuaded to acknowledge what had really occurred, and to give his reasons for wishing to keep the matter a secret. As for the lady Iijima, he intended, he said, to make her his wife as soon as possible.

'Oh, madness!' cried Yusai – losing all patience in the intensity of his alarm. 'Know, sir, that the people who have been coming here, night after night, are dead! Some frightful delusion is upon you! . . . Why, the simple fact that you long supposed O-Tsuyu to be dead, and repeated the *Nembutsu* for her, and made offerings before her tablet, is itself the proof! . . . The lips of the dead have touched you! – The hands of the dead have caressed you! . . . Even at this moment I see in your face the signs of death– and you will not believe! . . . Listen to me now, sir, I beg of you – if you wish to save yourself: otherwise you have less than twenty days to live. They told you – those people – that they were residing in the district of Shitaya, in Yanaka-no-Sasaki. Did you ever visit them at that place? No! – of course you did not! Then go today – as soon as you can – to Yanaka-no-Sasaki, and try to find their home! . . . '

And having uttered this counsel with the most vehement earnestness, Hakuodo Yusai abruptly took his departure.

Shinzaburo, startled though not convinced, resolved after a moment's reflection to follow the advice of the *ninsomi*, and to go to Shitaya. It was yet early in the morning when he reached the quarter of Yanaka-no-Sasaki, and began his search for the dwelling of O-Tsuyu. He went through every street and side-street, read all the names inscribed at the various entrances, and made inquiries whenever an opportunity presented itself. But he could not find anything resembling the little house mentioned by O-Yone; and none of the people whom he questioned knew of any house in the quarter inhabited by two single women. Feeling at last certain that further research would be useless, he turned homeward by the shortest way, which happened to lead through the grounds of the temple Shin-Banzui-In.

Suddenly his attention was attracted by two new tombs, placed side by side, at the rear of the temple. One was a common tomb, such as might have been erected for a person of humble rank: the other was a large and handsome monument; and hanging before it was a beautiful peony-lantern, which had probably been left there at the time of the Festival of the Dead. Shinzaburo remembered that the peony-lantern carried by O-Yone was exactly similar; and the coincidence impressed him as strange. He looked again at the tombs; but the tombs explained nothing. Neither bore any personal name – only the Buddhist *kaimyo*, or posthumous appellation. Then he determined to seek information at the temple. An acolyte stated, in reply to his questions, that the large tomb had been recently erected for the daughter of Iijima Heizayemon, the *hatamoto* of Ushigome; and that the small tomb next to it was that of her servant O-Yone, who had died of grief soon after the young lady's funeral.

Immediately to Shinzaburo's memory there recurred, with another and sinister meaning, the words of O-Yone: *'We went away, and found a very small house in Yanaka-no-Sasaki. There we are now just barely able to live – by doing a little private work* . . . ' Here was indeed the very small house – and in Yanaka-no-Sasaki. But the little *private work* . . . ?

Terror-stricken, the samurai hastened with all speed to the house of Yusai, and begged for his counsel and assistance. But Yusai declared himself unable to be of any aid in such a case. All that he could do was to send Shinzaburo to the high-priest Ryoseki, of Shin-Banzui-In, with a letter praying for immediate religious help.

7

The high-priest Ryoseki was a learned and a holy man. By spiritual vision he was able to know the secret of any sorrow, and the nature of the karma that had caused it. He heard unmoved the story of Shinzaburo, and said to him: 'A very great danger now threatens you, because of an error committed in one of your former states of existence. The karma that binds you to the dead is very strong; but if I tried to explain its character, you would not be able to understand. I shall therefore tell you only this – that the dead person has no desire to injure you out of hate, feels no enmity towards you: she is influenced, on the contrary, by the most passionate affection for you. Probably the girl has been in love with you from a time long preceding your present life – from a time of not less than three or four past existences; and it would seem that, although necessarily changing her form and condition at each succeeding birth, she has not been able to cease from following after you. Therefore it will not be an easy thing to escape from her influence . . . But now I am going to lend you this powerful *mamori*.[1] It is a pure gold image of that Buddha called the Sea-Sounding Tathagata – *Kai-On-Nyorai* – because his preaching of the Law sounds through the world like the sound of the sea. And this little image is especially a *shiryo-yoke*[2] –

---

1 The Japanese word *mamori* has significations at least as numerous as those attaching to our own term 'amulet'. It would be impossible, in a mere footnote, even to suggest the variety of Japanese religious objects to which the name is given. In this instance, the *mamori* is a very small image, probably enclosed in a miniature shrine of lacquer-work or metal, over which a silk cover is drawn. Such little images were often worn by samurai on the person. I was recently shown a miniature figure of Kwannon, in an iron case, which had been carried by an officer through the Satsuma war. He observed, with good reason, that it had probably saved his life; for it had stopped a bullet of which the dent was plainly visible.

2 From *shiryo*, a ghost, and *yokeru*, to exclude. The Japanese have two kinds of ghosts proper in their folk-lore: the spirits of the dead, *shiryo*; and the spirits of the living, *ikiryo*. A house or a person may be haunted by an *ikiryo* as well as by a *shiryo*.

which protects the living from the dead. This you must wear, in its covering, next to your body – under the girdle . . . Besides, I shall presently perform in the temple, a *Segaki*-service [1] for the repose of the troubled spirit . . . And here is a holy sutra, called *Ubo-Darani-Kyo*, or 'Treasure-Raining Sutra'; [2] you must be careful to recite it every night in your house – without fail . . . Furthermore I shall give you this package of *o-fuda* [3] – you must paste one of them over every opening of your house – no matter how small. If you do this, the power of the holy texts will prevent the dead from entering. But – whatever may happen – do not fail to recite the sutra.'

Shinzaburo humbly thanked the high-priest; and then, taking with him the image, the sutra, and the bundle of sacred texts, he made all haste to reach his home before the hour of sunset.

8

With Yusai's advice and help, Shinzaburo was able before dark to fix the holy texts over all the apertures of his dwelling. Then the *ninsomi* returned to his own house – leaving the youth alone. Night came, warm and clear. Shinzaburo made fast the doors, bound the precious amulet about his waist, entered his mosquito-net, and by the glow of a night-lantern began to recite the *Ubo-Darani-Kyo*. For a long time he chanted the words, comprehending little of their meaning – then he tried to obtain some rest. But his mind was still too much disturbed by the strange events of the day. Midnight passed; and no sleep came to him. At last he

1 A special service – accompanying offerings of food, etc., to those dead having no living relatives or friends to care for them – is thus termed. In this case, however, the service would be of a particular and exceptional kind.
2 The name would be more correctly written *Uho-Darani-Kyo*. It is the Japanese pronunciation of the title of a very short sutra translated out of Sanscrit into Chinese by the Indian priest Amoghavajra, probably during the eighth century. The Chinese text contains transliterations of some mysterious Sanscrit words – apparently talismanic words – like those to be seen in Kern's translation of the Saddharma-Pundarika, ch. xxvi.
3 *O-fuda* is the general name given to religious texts used as charms or talismans. They are sometimes stamped or burned upon wood, but more commonly written or printed upon narrow strips of paper. *O-fuda* are pasted above house-entrances, on the walls of rooms, upon tablets placed in household shrines, etc., etc. Some kinds are worn about the person – others are made into pellets, and swallowed as spiritual medicine. The text of the larger *o-fuda* is often accompanied by curious pictures or symbolic illustrations.

heard the boom of the great temple-bell of Dentsu-In announcing the eighth hour.[1]

It ceased; and Shinzaburo suddenly heard the sound of *geta* approaching from the old direction – but this time more slowly: *karan-koron, karan-koron*! At once a cold sweat broke over his forehead. Opening the sutra hastily, with trembling hand, he began again to recite it aloud. The steps came nearer and nearer – reached the live hedge – stopped! Then, strange to say, Shinzaburo felt unable to remain under his mosquito-net: something stronger even than his fear impelled him to look; and, instead of continuing to recite the *Ubo-Darani-Kyo*, he foolishly approached the shutters, and through a chink peered out into the night. Before the house he saw O-Tsuyu standing, and O-Yone with the peony-lantern; and both of them were gazing at the Buddhist texts pasted above the entrance. Never before – not even in what time she lived – had O-Tsuyu appeared so beautiful; and Shinzaburo felt his heart drawn towards her with a power almost resistless. But the terror of death and the terror of the unknown restrained; and there went on within him such a struggle between his love and his fear that he became as one suffering in the body the pains of the *Sho-netsu* hell.[2]

Presently he heard the voice of the maid-servant, saying: 'My dear mistress, there is no way to enter. The heart of Hagiwara Sama must have changed. For the promise that he made last night has been broken; and the doors have been made fast to keep us out . . . We cannot go in tonight . . . It will be wiser for you to make up your mind not to think any more about him, because his feeling towards you has certainly changed. It is evident that he does not want to see you. So it will be better not to give yourself any more trouble for the sake of a man whose heart is so unkind.'

But the girl answered, weeping: 'Oh, to think that this could happen after the pledges which we made to each other! . . . Often I was told that the heart of a man changes as quickly as the sky of autumn – yet surely the heart of Hagiwara Sama cannot be so cruel

1 According to the old Japanese way of counting time, this *yatsudoki* or eighth hour was the same as our two o'clock in the morning. Each Japanese hour was equal to two European hours, so that there were only six hours instead of our twelve; and these six hours were counted backwards in the order – 9, 8, 7, 6, 5, 4. Thus the ninth hour corresponded to our midday, or midnight; half-past nine to our one o'clock; eight to our two o'clock. Two o'clock in the morning, also called 'the Hour of the Ox', was the Japanese hour of ghosts and goblins.

2 *En-netsu* or *Sho-netsu* (Sanscrit 'Tapana') is the sixth of the Eight Hot Hells of Japanese Buddhism. One day of life in this hell is equal in duration to thousands (some say millions) of human years.

that he should really intend to exclude me in this way! . . . Dear Yone, please find some means of taking me to him . . . Unless you do, I will never, never go home again.'

Thus she continued to plead, veiling her face with her long sleeves – and very beautiful she looked, and very touching; but the fear of death was strong upon her lover.

O-Yone at last made answer – 'My dear young lady, why will you trouble your mind about a man who seems to be so cruel? . . . Well, let us see if there be no way to enter at the back of the house: come with me!'

And taking O-Tsuyu by the hand, she led her away toward the rear of the dwelling; and there the two disappeared as suddenly as the light disappears when the flame of a lamp is blown out.

9

Night after night the shadows came at the Hour of the Ox; and nightly Shinzaburo heard the weeping of O-Tsuyu. Yet he believed himself saved – little imagining that his doom had already been decided by the character of his dependents.

Tomozo had promised Yusai never to speak to any other person – not even to O-Mine– of the strange events that were taking place. But Tomozo was not long suffered by the haunters to rest in peace. Night after night O-Yone entered into his dwelling, and roused him from his sleep, and asked him to remove the *o-fuda* placed over one very small window at the back of his master's house. And Tomozo, out of fear, as often promised her to take away the *o-fuda* before the next sundown; but never by day could he make up his mind to remove it – believing that evil was intended to Shinzaburo. At last, in a night of storm, O-Yone startled him from slumber with a cry of reproach, and stooped above his pillow, and said to him: 'Have a care how you trifle with us! If, by tomorrow night, you do not take away that text, you shall learn how I can hate!' And she made her face so frightful as she spoke that Tomozo nearly died of terror.

O-Mine, the wife of Tomozo, had never till then known of these visits: even to her husband they had seemed like bad dreams. But on this particular night it chanced that, waking suddenly, she heard the voice of a woman talking to Tomozo. Almost in the same moment the talking ceased; and when O-Mine looked about her, she saw, by the light of the night-lamp, only her husband – shuddering and white with fear. The stranger was gone; the doors were fast: it seemed impossible that anybody could have entered. Nevertheless the jealousy of the wife had been aroused; and she began to chide and to question Tomozo in such a manner that he thought himself obliged to betray the secret, and to explain the terrible dilemma in which he had been placed.

Then the passion of O-Mine yielded to wonder and alarm; but she was a subtle woman, and she devised immediately a plan to save her husband by the sacrifice of her master. And she gave Tomozo a cunning counsel – telling him to make conditions with the dead.

They came again on the following night at the Hour of the Ox; and O-Mine hid herself on hearing the sound of their coming – *karan-koron, karan-koron*! But Tomozo went out to meet them in the dark, and even found courage to say to them what his wife had told him to say: 'It is true that I deserve your blame – but I had no wish to cause you anger. The reason that the *o-fuda* has not been taken away is that my wife and I are able to live only by the help of Hagiwara Sama, and that we cannot expose him to any danger without bringing misfortune upon ourselves. But if we could obtain the sum of a hundred *ryo* in gold, we should be able to please you, because we should then need no help from anybody. Therefore if you will give us a hundred *ryo*, I can take the *o-fuda* away without being afraid of losing our only means of support.'

When he had uttered these words, O-Yone and O-Tsuyu looked at each other in silence for a moment. Then O-Yone said: 'Mistress, I told you that it was not right to trouble this man – as we have no just cause of ill-will against him. But it is certainly useless to fret yourself about Hagiwara Sama, because his heart has changed towards you. Now once again, my dear young lady, let me beg you not to think any more about him!'

But O-Tsuyu, weeping, made answer: 'Dear Yone, whatever may happen, I cannot possibly keep myself from thinking about him! You know that you can get a hundred *ryo* to have the *o-fuda* taken off . . . Only once more, I pray, dear Yone! – Only once more bring me face to face with Hagiwara Sama – I beseech you!' And hiding her face with her sleeve, she thus continued to plead.

'Oh! why will you ask me to do these things?' responded O-Yone. 'You know very well that I have no money. But since you will persist in this whim of yours, in spite of all that I can say, I suppose that I must try to find the money somehow, and to bring it here tomorrow night . . .' Then, turning to the faithless Tomozo, she said: 'Tomozo, I must tell you that Hagiwara Sama now wears upon his body a *mamori* called by the name of *Kai-On-Nyorai*, and that so long as he wears it we cannot approach him. So you will have to get that *mamori* away from him, by some means or other, as well as to remove the *o-fuda*.'

Tomozo feebly made answer: 'That also I can do, if you will promise to bring me the hundred *ryo*.'

'Well, mistress,' said O-Yone, 'you will wait – will you not – until tomorrow night?'

'Oh, dear Yone!' sobbed the other – 'have we to go back tonight again without seeing Hagiwara Sama? Ah! it is cruel!'

And the shadow of the mistress, weeping, was led away by the shadow of the maid.

10

Another day went, and another night came, and the dead came with it. But this time no lamentation was heard without the house of Hagiwara; for the faithless servant found his reward at the Hour of the Ox, and removed the *o-fuda*. Moreover he had been able, while his master was at the bath, to steal from its case the golden *mamori*, and to substitute for it an image of copper; and he had buried the *Kai-On-Nyorai* in a desolate field. So the visitants found nothing to oppose their entering. Veiling their faces with their sleeves they rose and passed, like a streaming of vapour, into the little window from over which the holy text had been torn away. But what happened thereafter within the house Tomozo never knew.

The sun was high before he ventured again to approach his master's dwelling, and to knock upon the sliding-doors. For the first time in years he obtained no response; and the silence made him afraid. Repeatedly he called, and received no answer. Then, aided by O-Mine, he succeeded in effecting an entrance and making his way alone to the sleeping-room, where he called again in vain. He rolled back the rumbling shutters to admit the light; but still within the house there was no stir. At last he dared to lift a corner of the mosquito-net. But no sooner had he looked beneath than he fled from the house, with a cry of horror.

Shinzaburo was dead – hideously dead – and his face was the face of a man who had died in the uttermost agony of fear – and lying beside him in the bed were the bones of a woman! And the bones of the arms, and the bones of the hands, clung fast about his neck.

II

Hakuodo Yusai, the fortune-teller, went to view the corpse at the prayer of the faithless Tomozo. The old man was terrified and astonished at the spectacle, but looked about him with a keen eye. He soon perceived that the *o-fuda* had been taken from the little window at the back of the house; and on searching the body of Shinzaburo, he discovered that the golden *mamori* had been taken from its wrapping, and a copper image of Fudo put in place of it. He suspected Tomozo of the theft; but the whole occurrence was so very extraordinary that he thought it prudent to consult with the priest Ryoseki before taking further action. Therefore, after having made a careful examination of the premises, he betook himself to the temple Shin-Banzui-In, as quickly as his aged limbs could bear him.

Ryoseki, without waiting to hear the purpose of the old man's visit, at once invited him into a private apartment.

'You know that you are always welcome here,' said Ryoseki. 'Please seat yourself at ease . . . Well, I am sorry to tell you that Hagiwara Sama is dead.'

Yusai wonderingly exclaimed: 'Yes, he is dead – but how did you learn of it?'

The priest responded: 'Hagiwara Sama was suffering from the results of an evil karma; and his attendant was a bad man. What happened to Hagiwara Sama was unavoidable – his destiny had been determined from a time long before his last birth. It will be better for you not to let your mind be troubled by this event.'

Yusai said: 'I have heard that a priest of pure life may gain power to see into the future for a hundred years; but truly this is the first time in my existence that I have had proof of such power . . . Still, there is another matter about which I am very anxious . . .'

'You mean,' interrupted Ryoseki, 'the stealing of the holy *mamori*, the *Kai-On-Nyorai*. But you must not give yourself any concern about that. The image has been buried in a field; and it will be found there and returned to me during the eighth month of the coming year. So please do not be anxious about it.'

More and more amazed, the old *ninsomi* ventured to observe: 'I have studied the *In-Yo*,'[1] and the science of divination; and I make

1 The Male and Female principles of the universe, the Active and Passive forces of Nature. Yusai refers here to the old Chinese nature-philosophy – better known to Western readers by the name *Feng-Shui*.

my living by telling peoples' fortunes – but I cannot possibly understand how you know these things.'

Ryoseki answered gravely: 'Never mind how I happen to know
them . . . I now want to speak to you about Hagiwara's funeral. The
House of Hagiwara has its own family-cemetery, of course; but
to bury him there would not be proper. He must be buried beside
O-Tsuyu, the Lady Iijima; for his karma-relation to her was a very
deep one. And it is but right that you should erect a tomb for him
at your own cost, because you have been indebted to him for many
favours.'

Thus it came to pass that Shinzaburo was buried beside O-Tsuyu, in
the cemetery of Shin-Banzui-In, in Yanaka-no-Sasaki.

Here ends the story of the Ghosts in the
Romance of the Peony-Lantern.

*   *   *

My friend asked me whether the story had interested me; and I
answered by telling him that I wanted to go to the cemetery of Shin-
Banzui-In – so as to realise more definitely the local colour of the
author's studies.

'I shall go with you at once,' he said. 'But what did you think of the
personages?'

'To Western thinking,' I made answer, 'Shinzaburo is a despicable
creature. I have been mentally comparing him with the true lovers of
our old ballad-literature. They were only too glad to follow a dead
sweetheart into the grave; and nevertheless, being Christians, they
believed that they had only one human life to enjoy in this world.
But Shinzaburo was a Buddhist – with a million lives behind him
and a million lives before him; and he was too selfish to give up even
one miserable existence for the sake of the girl that came back to
him from the dead. Then he was even more cowardly than selfish.
Although a samurai by birth and training, he had to beg a priest to
save him from ghosts. In every way he proved himself contemptible;
and O-Tsuyu did quite right in choking him to death.'

'From the Japanese point of view, likewise,' my friend responded,
'Shinzaburo is rather contemptible. But the use of this weak character helped the author to develop incidents that could not otherwise, perhaps, have been so effectively managed. To my thinking,
the only attractive character in the story is that of O-Yone: type of

the old-time loyal and loving servant – intelligent, shrewd, full of resource – faithful not only unto death, but beyond death . . . Well, let us go to Shin-Banzui-In.'

We found the temple uninteresting, and the cemetery an abomination of desolation. Spaces once occupied by graves had been turned into potato-patches. Between were tombs leaning at all angles out of the perpendicular, tablets made illegible by scurf, empty pedestals, shattered water-tanks, and statues of Buddhas without heads or hands. Recent rains had soaked the black soil – leaving here and there small pools of slime about which swarms of tiny frogs were hopping. Everything – excepting the potato-patches – seemed to have been neglected for years. In a shed just within the gate, we observed a woman cooking; and my companion presumed to ask her if she knew anything about the tombs described in the Romance of the Peony-Lantern.

'Ah! the tombs of O-Tsuyu and O-Yone?' she responded, smiling – 'you will find them near the end of the first row at the back of the temple – next to the statue of Jizo.'

Surprises of this kind I had met with elsewhere in Japan.

We picked our way between the rain-pools and between the green ridges of young potatoes – whose roots were doubtless feeding on the substance of many another O-Tsuyu and O-Yone – and we reached at last two lichen-eaten tombs of which the inscriptions seemed almost obliterated. Beside the larger tomb was a statue of Jizo, with a broken nose.

'The characters are not easy to make out,' said my friend – 'but wait!' . . . He drew from his sleeve a sheet of soft white paper, laid it over the inscription, and began to rub the paper with a lump of clay. As he did so, the characters appeared in white on the blackened surface.

'*Eleventh day, third month – rat, Elder Brother, Fire – sixth year of Horeki* [A.D. 1756]' . . . This would seem to be the grave of some innkeeper of Nedzu, named Kichibei. Let us see what is on the other monument.'

With a fresh sheet of paper he presently brought out the text of a kaimyo, and read: '*En-myo-In, Ho-yo-I-tei-ken-shi, Ho-ni*': '*Nun-of-the-Law, Illustrious, Pure-of-heart-and-will, Famed-in-the-Law – inhabiting the Mansion-of-the-Preaching-of-Wonder*' . . . 'The grave of some Buddhist nun.'

'What utter humbug!' I exclaimed. 'That woman was only making fun of us.'

'Now,' my friend protested, 'you are unjust to the woman! You came here because you wanted a sensation; and she tried her very best to please you. You did not suppose that ghost-story was true, did you?'

SOME CHINESE GHOSTS

To my friend
HENRY EDWARD KREHBIEL
THE MUSICIAN

Who, speaking the speech of melody
unto the children of Tien-Hia –
unto the wandering Tsing-Jin,
whose skins have the colour of gold –
moved them to make strange sounds
upon the serpent-bellied san-hien;
persuaded them to play for me
upon the shrieking ya-hien;
prevailed on them to sing me
a song of their native land –
the song of Mohli-Hwa,
the song of the jasmine-flower

PREFACE

I think that my best apology for the insignificant size of this volume is the very character of the material composing it. In preparing the legends I sought especially for *weird beauty*; and I could not forget this striking observation in Sir Walter Scott's 'Essay on Imitations of the Ancient Ballad': 'The supernatural, though appealing to certain powerful emotions very widely and deeply sown amongst the human race, is, nevertheless, *a spring which is peculiarly apt to lose its elasticity by being too much pressed upon.*'

Those desirous to familiarise themselves with Chinese literature as a whole have had the way made smooth for them by the labours of linguists like Julien, Pavie, Rémusat, De Rosny, Schlegel, Legge, Hervey-Saint-Denys, Williams, Biot, Giles, Wylie, Beal, and many other Sinologists. To such great explorers, indeed, the realm of Cathayan story belongs by right of discovery and conquest; yet the humbler traveller who follows wonderingly after them into the vast and mysterious pleasure-grounds of Chinese fancy may surely be permitted to cull a few of the marvellous flowers there growing – a self-luminous *hwa-wang*, a black lily, a phosphoric rose or two – as souvenirs of his curious voyage.

L.H.
New Orleans
March 15, 1886

THE SOUL OF THE
GREAT BELL

*She hath spoken, and her words
still resound in his ears.*

HAO-KHIEOU-TCHOUAN: C. ix

The Soul of the Great Bell

The water-clock marks the hour in the *Ta-chung sz'* – in the Tower of the Great Bell: now the mallet is lifted to smite the lips of the metal monster – the vast lips inscribed with Buddhist texts from the sacred *Fa-hwa-King*, from the chapters of the holy *Ling-yen-King*! Hear the great bell responding! – How mighty her voice, though tongueless! – *KO-NGAI*! All the little dragons on the high-tilted eaves of the green roofs shiver to the tips of their gilded tails under that deep wave of sound; all the porcelain gargoyles tremble on their carven perches; all the hundred little bells of the pagodas quiver with desire to speak. *KO-NGAI*! – All the green-and-gold tiles of the temple are vibrating; the wooden goldfish above them are writhing against the sky; the uplifted finger of Fo shakes high over the heads of the worshippers through the blue fog of incense! *KO-NGAI*! – What a thunder tone was that! All the lacquered goblins on the palace cornices wriggle their fire-coloured tongues! And after each huge shock, how wondrous the multiple echo and the great golden moan and, at last, the sudden sibilant sobbing in the ears when the immense tone faints away in broken whispers of silver – as though a woman should whisper, '*Hiai*!' Even so the great bell hath sounded every day for well-nigh five hundred years – *Ko-Ngai*: first with stupendous clang, then with immeasurable moan of gold, then with silver murmuring of '*Hiai*!' And there is not a child in all the many-coloured ways of the old Chinese city who does not know the story of the great bell – who cannot tell you why the great bell says *Ko-Ngai* and *Hiai*!

* * *

Now, this is the story of the great bell in the *Ta-chung sz'*, as the same is related in the *Pe-Hiao-Tou-Choue*, written by the learned Yu-Pao-Tchen, of the City of Kwang-tchau-fu.

Nearly five hundred years ago the Celestially August, the Son of Heaven, Yong-Lo, of the 'Illustrious', or Ming, dynasty, commanded the worthy official Kouan-Yu that he should have a bell made of such size that the sound thereof might be heard for one hundred *li*. And he further ordained that the voice of the bell should be strengthened with brass, and deepened with gold, and sweetened with silver; and that the face and the great lips of it should be graven with blessed sayings from the sacred books, and that it should be suspended in the centre of the imperial capital, to sound through all the many-coloured ways of the City of Peking.

Therefore the worthy mandarin Kouan-Yu assembled the master-moulders and the renowned bellsmiths of the empire, and all men of great repute and cunning in foundry work; and they measured the materials for the alloy, and treated them skilfully, and prepared the moulds, the fires, the instruments, and the monstrous melting-pot for fusing the metal. And they laboured exceedingly, like giants – neglecting only rest and sleep and the comforts of life; toiling both night and day in obedience to Kouan-Yu, and striving in all things to do the behest of the Son of Heaven.

But when the metal had been cast, and the earthen mould separated from the glowing casting, it was discovered that, despite their great labour and ceaseless care, the result was void of worth; for the metals had rebelled one against the other – the gold had scorned alliance with the brass, the silver would not mingle with the molten iron. Therefore the moulds had to be once more prepared, the fires rekindled, and the metal remelted, and all the work tediously and toilsomely repeated. The Son of Heaven heard, and was angry, but spake nothing.

A second time the bell was cast, and the result was even worse. Still the metals obstinately refused to blend one with the other; and there was no uniformity in the bell, and the sides of it were cracked and fissured, and the lips of it were slagged and split asunder; so that all the labour had to be repeated even a third time, to the great dismay of Kouan-Yu. And when the Son of Heaven heard these things, he was angrier than before; and sent his messenger to Kouan-Yu with a letter, written upon lemon-coloured silk, and sealed with the seal of the Dragon, containing these words:

From the Mighty Yong-Lo, the Sublime Tait-Sung, the Celestial and August – whose reign is called 'Ming' – to Kouan-Yu the Fuh-yin:

Twice thou hast betrayed the trust we have deigned graciously to place in thee; if thou fail a third time in fulfilling our command, thy head shall be severed from thy neck. Tremble, and obey.

*   *   *

Now, Kouan-Yu had a daughter of dazzling loveliness, whose name – Ko-Ngai – was ever in the mouths of poets, and whose heart was even more beautiful than her face. Ko-Ngai loved her father with such love that she had refused a hundred worthy suitors rather than make his home desolate by her absence; and when she had seen the awful yellow missive, sealed with the Dragon-Seal, she fainted away with fear for her father's sake. And when her senses and her strength returned to her, she could not rest or sleep for thinking of her parent's danger, until she had secretly sold some of her jewels, and with the money so obtained had hastened to an astrologer, and paid him a great price to advise her by what means her father might be saved from the peril impending over him. So the astrologer made observations of the heavens, and marked the aspect of the Silver Stream (which we call the Milky Way), and examined the signs of the Zodiac – the *Hwang-tao*, or Yellow Road – and consulted the table of the Five *Hin*, or Principles of the Universe, and the mystical books of the alchemists. And after a long silence, he made answer to her, saying: 'Gold and brass will never meet in wedlock, silver and iron never will embrace, until the flesh of a maiden be melted in the crucible; until the blood of a virgin be mixed with the metals in their fusion.' So Ko-Ngai returned home sorrowful at heart; but she kept secret all that she had heard, and told no-one what she had done.

*   *   *

At last came the awful day when the third and last effort to cast the great bell was to be made; and Ko-Ngai, together with her waiting-woman, accompanied her father to the foundry, and they took their places upon a platform overlooking the toiling of the moulders and the lava of liquefied metal. All the workmen wrought their tasks in silence; there was no sound heard but the muttering of the fires. And the muttering deepened into a roar like the roar of typhoons approaching, and the blood-red lake of metal slowly brightened like the vermilion of a sunrise, and the vermilion was transmuted into a radiant glow of gold, and the gold whitened blindingly, like the silver face of a full moon. Then the workers ceased to feed the raving flame, and all fixed their eyes upon the eyes of Kouan-Yu; and Kouan-Yu prepared to give the signal to cast.

But ere ever he lifted his finger, a cry caused him to turn his head; and all heard the voice of Ko-Ngai sounding sharply sweet as a bird's

song above the great thunder of the fires – '*For thy sake, O my Father!*'
And even as she cried, she leaped into the white flood of metal; and
the lava of the furnace roared to receive her, and spattered monstrous flakes of flame to the roof, and burst over the verge of the
earthen crater, and cast up a whirling fountain of many-coloured
fires, and subsided quakingly, with lightnings and with thunders and
with mutterings.

Then the father of Ko-Ngai, wild with his grief, would have
leaped in after her, but that strong men held him back and kept
firm grasp upon him until he had fainted away and they could bear
him like one dead to his home. And the serving-woman of Ko-
Ngai, dizzy and speechless for pain, stood before the furnace, still
holding in her hands a shoe, a tiny, dainty shoe, with embroidery
of pearls and flowers – the shoe of her beautiful mistress that
was. For she had sought to grasp Ko-Ngai by the foot as she leaped,
but had only been able to clutch the shoe, and the pretty shoe
came off in her hand; and she continued to stare at it like one
gone mad.

But in spite of all these things, the command of the Celestial
and August had to be obeyed, and the work of the moulders to
be finished, hopeless as the result might be. Yet the glow of the metal
seemed purer and whiter than before; and there was no sign of the
beautiful body that had been entombed therein. So the ponderous
casting was made; and lo! when the metal had become cool, it was
found that the bell was beautiful to look upon, and perfect in form,
and wonderful in colour above all other bells. Nor was there any
trace found of the body of Ko-Ngai; for it had been totally absorbed
by the precious alloy, and blended with the well-blended brass
and gold, with the intermingling of the silver and the iron. And
when they sounded the bell, its tones were found to be deeper and
mellower and mightier than the tones of any other bell – reaching
even beyond the distance of one hundred *li*, like a pealing of summer
thunder; and yet also like some vast voice uttering a name, a woman's
name – the name of Ko-Ngai!

*   *   *

And still, between each mighty stroke there is a long low moaning
heard; and ever the moaning ends with a sound of sobbing and of
complaining, as though a weeping woman should murmur, '*Hiai*!'
And still, when the people hear that great golden moan they keep
silence; but when the sharp, sweet shuddering comes in the air, and

the sobbing of '*Hiai*!' then, indeed, all the Chinese mothers in all the many-coloured ways of Peking whisper to their little ones: '*Listen! That is Ko-Ngai crying for her shoe! That is Ko-Ngai calling for her shoe!*'

THE STORY OF MING-Y

THE ANCIENT WORDS OF KOUEI — MASTER OF MUSICIANS
IN THE COURTS OF THE EMPEROR YAO

When ye make to resound the stone melodious,
the Ming-Khieou —
When ye touch the lyre that is called Kin,
or the guitar that is called Ssé —
Accompanying their sound with song —
Then do the grandfather and the father return;
Then do the ghosts of the ancestors come to hear.

The Story of Ming-Y

Sang the Poet Tching-Kou: 'Surely the Peach-Flowers blossom over the tomb of Sie-Thao.'

Do you ask me who she was – the beautiful Sie-Thao? For a thousand years and more the trees have been whispering above her bed of stone. And the syllables of her name come to the listener with the lisping of the leaves; with the quivering of many-fingered boughs; with the fluttering of lights and shadows; with the breath, sweet as a woman's presence, of numberless savage flowers – *Sie-Thao*. But, saving the whispering of her name, what the trees say cannot be understood; and they alone remember the years of Sie-Thao. Something about her you might, nevertheless, learn from any of those *Kiang-kou-jin* – those famous Chinese story-tellers, who nightly narrate to listening crowds, in consideration of a few *tsien*, the legends of the past. Something concerning her you may also find in the book entitled *Kin-Kou-Ki-Koan*, which signifies in our tongue: 'The Marvellous Happenings of Ancient and of Recent Times'. And perhaps of all things therein written, the most marvellous is this memory of Sie-Thao:

Five hundred years ago, in the reign of the Emperor Houng-Wou, whose dynasty was *Ming*, there lived in the City of Genii, the city of Kwang-tchau-fu, a man celebrated for his learning and for his piety, named Tien-Pelou. This Tien-Pelou had one son, a beautiful boy, who for scholarship and for bodily grace and for polite accomplishments had no superior among the youths of his age. And his name was Ming-Y.

Now when the lad was in his eighteenth summer, it came to pass that Pelou, his father, was appointed Inspector of Public Instruction at the city of Tching-tou; and Ming-Y accompanied his parents thither. Near the city of Tching-tou lived a rich man of rank, a high commissioner of the government, whose name was Tchang, and who wanted to find a worthy teacher for his children. On hearing of the arrival of the new Inspector of Public Instruction, the noble Tchang visited him to obtain advice in this matter; and happening to meet and converse with Pelou's accomplished son, immediately engaged Ming-Y as a private tutor for his family.

Now as the house of this Lord Tchang was situated several miles from town, it was deemed best that Ming-Y should abide in the house of his employer. Accordingly the youth made ready all things necessary for his new sojourn; and his parents, bidding him farewell, counselled him wisely, and cited to him the words of Lao-tsu and of the ancient sages:

'*By a beautiful face the world is filled with love; but Heaven may never be deceived thereby. Shouldst thou behold a woman coming from the East, look thou to the West; shouldst thou perceive a maiden approaching from the West, turn thine eyes to the East.*'

If Ming-Y did not heed this counsel in after days, it was only because of his youth and the thoughtlessness of a naturally joyous heart.

And he departed to abide in the house of Lord Tchang, while the autumn passed, and the winter also.

* * *

When the time of the second moon of spring was drawing near, and that happy day which the Chinese call *Hoa-tchao*, or, 'The Birthday of a Hundred Flowers', a longing came upon Ming-Y to see his parents; and he opened his heart to the good Tchang, who not only gave him the permission he desired, but also pressed into his hand a silver gift of two ounces, thinking that the lad might wish to bring some little memento to his father and mother. For it is the Chinese custom, on the feast of Hoa-tchao, to make presents to friends and relations.

That day all the air was drowsy with blossom perfume, and vibrant with the droning of bees. It seemed to Ming-Y that the path he followed had not been trodden by any other for many long years; the grass was tall upon it; vast trees on either side interlocked their mighty and moss-grown arms above him, beshadowing the way; but the leafy obscurities quivered with bird-song, and the deep vistas of the wood were glorified by vapours of gold, and odorous with flower-breathings as a temple with incense. The dreamy joy of the day entered into the heart of Ming-Y; and he sat him down among the young blossoms, under the branches swaying against the violet sky, to drink in the perfume and the light, and to enjoy the great sweet silence. Even while thus reposing, a sound caused him to turn his eyes toward a shady place where wild peach-trees were in bloom; and he beheld a young woman, beautiful as the pinkening blossoms themselves, trying to hide among them. Though he looked for a moment only, Ming-Y could not avoid discerning the loveliness of her face, the golden purity of her complexion, and the brightness of her long eyes, that sparkled under a pair of brows as daintily curved as the wings of the silkworm butterfly outspread. Ming-Y at once turned his gaze away, and, rising quickly, proceeded on his journey. But so much embarrassed did he feel at the idea of those charming eyes peeping at him through the leaves, that he suffered the money he had been carrying in his sleeve to fall, without being aware of it. A few moments later he heard the patter of light feet running behind him, and a woman's voice calling him by name. Turning his face in great surprise, he saw a comely servant-maid, who said to him, 'Sir, my mistress bade me pick up and return you this silver which you dropped upon the road.' Ming-Y thanked the girl gracefully, and requested her to convey his compliments to her mistress. Then he proceeded on his way through the perfumed silence, athwart the shadows that dreamed along the forgotten path, dreaming himself also, and feeling his heart beating with strange quickness at the thought of the beautiful being that he had seen.

* * *

It was just such another day when Ming-Y, returning by the same path, paused once more at the spot where the gracious figure had momentarily appeared before him. But this time he was surprised to perceive, through a long vista of immense trees, a dwelling that had previously escaped his notice – a country residence, not large, yet elegant to an unusual degree. The bright blue tiles of its curved and serrated double roof, rising above the foliage, seemed to blend their colour with the luminous azure of the day; the green-and-gold designs of its carven porticos were exquisite artistic mockeries of leaves and flowers bathed in sunshine. And at the summit of terrace-steps before it, guarded by great porcelain tortoises, Ming-Y saw standing the mistress of the mansion – the idol of his passionate fancy – accompanied by the same waiting-maid who had borne to her his message of gratitude. While Ming-Y looked, he perceived that their eyes were upon him; they smiled and conversed together as if speaking about him; and, shy though he was, the youth found courage to salute the fair one from a distance. To his astonishment, the young servant beckoned him to approach; and opening a rustic gate half veiled by trailing plants bearing crimson flowers, Ming-Y advanced along the verdant alley leading to the terrace, with mingled feelings of surprise and timid joy. As he drew near, the beautiful lady withdrew from sight; but the maid waited at the broad steps to receive him, and said as he ascended: 'Sir, my mistress understands you wish to thank her for the trifling service she recently bade me do you, and requests that you will enter the house, as she knows you already by repute, and desires to have the pleasure of bidding you good-day.'

Ming-Y entered bashfully, his feet making no sound upon a matting elastically soft as forest moss, and found himself in a reception-chamber vast, cool, and fragrant with scent of blossoms freshly gathered. A delicious quiet pervaded the mansion; shadows of flying birds passed over the bands of light that fell through the half-blinds of bamboo; great butterflies, with pinions of fiery colour, found their way in, to hover a moment about the painted vases, and pass out again into the mysterious woods. And noiselessly as they, the young mistress of the mansion entered by another door, and kindly greeted the boy, who lifted his hands to his breast and bowed low in salutation. She was taller than he had deemed her, and supplely-slender as a beauteous lily; her black hair was interwoven with the creamy blossoms of the *chu-sha-kih*; her robes of pale silk took shifting tints when she moved, as vapours change hue with the changing of the light.

'If I be not mistaken,' she said, when both had seated themselves after having exchanged the customary formalities of politeness, 'my honoured visitor is none other than Tien-chou, surnamed Ming-Y, educator of the children of my respected relative, the High Commissioner Tchang. As the family of Lord Tchang is my family also, I cannot but consider the teacher of his children as one of my own kin.'

'Lady,' replied Ming-Y, not a little astonished, 'may I dare to inquire the name of your honoured family, and to ask the relation which you hold to my noble patron?'

'The name of my poor family,' responded the comely lady, 'is *Ping* – an ancient family of the city of Tching-tou. I am the daughter of a certain Sie of Moun-hao; Sie is my name, likewise; and I was married to a young man of the Ping family, whose name was Khang. By this marriage I became related to your excellent patron; but my husband died soon after our wedding, and I have chosen this solitary place to reside in during the period of my widowhood.'

There was a drowsy music in her voice, as of the melody of brooks, the murmurings of spring; and such a strange grace in the manner of her speech as Ming-Y had never heard before. Yet, on learning that she was a widow, the youth would not have presumed to remain long in her presence without a formal invitation; and after having sipped the cup of rich tea presented to him, he arose to depart. Sie would not suffer him to go so quickly.

'Nay, friend,' she said; 'stay yet a little while in my house, I pray you; for, should your honoured patron ever learn that you had been here, and that I had not treated you as a respected guest, and regaled you even as I would him, I know that he would be greatly angered. Remain at least to supper.'

So Ming-Y remained, rejoicing secretly in his heart, for Sie seemed to him the fairest and sweetest being he had ever known, and he felt that he loved her even more than his father and his mother. And while they talked the long shadows of the evening slowly blended into one violet darkness; the great citron-light of the sunset faded out; and those starry beings that are called the Three Councillors, who preside over life and death and the destinies of men, opened their cold bright eyes in the northern sky. Within the mansion of Sie the painted lanterns were lighted; the table was laid for the evening repast; and Ming-Y took his place at it, feeling little inclination to eat, and thinking only of the charming face before him. Observing that he scarcely tasted the dainties laid upon his plate, Sie pressed her young guest to partake of wine; and they drank several cups together. It was a purple wine, so cool that the cup into which it was poured became covered with vapoury dew; yet it seemed to warm the veins with strange fire. To Ming-Y, as he drank, all things became more luminous as by enchantment; the walls of the chamber appeared to recede, and the roof to heighten; the lamps glowed like stars in their chains, and the voice of Sie floated to the boy's ears like some far melody heard through the spaces of a drowsy night. His heart swelled; his tongue loosened; and words flitted from his lips that he had fancied he could never dare to utter. Yet Sie sought not to restrain him; her lips gave no smile, but her long bright eyes seemed to laugh with pleasure at his words of praise, and to return his gaze of passionate admiration with affectionate interest.

'I have heard,' she said, 'of your rare talent, and of your many elegant accomplishments. I know how to sing a little, although I cannot claim to possess any musical learning; and now that I have the honour of finding myself in the society of a musical professor, I will venture to lay modesty aside, and beg you to sing a few songs with me. I should deem it no small gratification if you would condescend to examine my musical compositions.'

'The honour and the gratification, dear lady,' replied Ming-Y, 'will be mine; and I feel helpless to express the gratitude which the offer of so rare a favour deserves.'

The serving-maid, obedient to the summons of a little silver gong, brought in the music and retired. Ming-Y took the manuscripts, and began to examine them with eager delight. The paper upon which they were written had a pale yellow tint, and was light as a fabric of gossamer; but the characters were antiquely beautiful, as though they had been traced by the brush of Heisong Che-Tchoo himself – that divine Genius of Ink, who is no bigger than a fly; and the signatures attached to the compositions were the signatures of Youen-tchin, Kao-pien, and Thou-mou – mighty poets and musicians of the dynasty of Thang! Ming-Y could not repress a scream of delight at the sight of treasures so inestimable and so unique; scarcely could he summon resolution enough to permit them to leave his hands even for a moment. 'O Lady!' he cried, 'these are veritably priceless things, surpassing in worth the treasures of all kings. This indeed is the handwriting of those great masters who sang five hundred years before our birth. How marvellously it has been preserved! Is not this the wondrous ink of which it was written: *Po-nien-jou-chi*, *I-tien-jou-ki* – 'After centuries I remain firm as stone, and the letters that I make like lacquer'? And how divine the charm of this composition! – the song of Kao-pien, prince of poets, and Governor of Sze-tchouen five hundred years ago!'

'Kao-pien! Darling Kao-pien!' murmured Sie, with a singular light in her eyes. 'Kao-pien is also my favourite. Dear Ming-Y, let us chant his verses together, to the melody of old – the music of those grand years when men were nobler and wiser than today.'

And their voices rose through the perfumed night like the voices of the wonder-birds – of the Fung-hoang – blending together in liquid sweetness. Yet a moment, and Ming-Y, overcome by the witchery of his companion's voice, could only listen in speechless ecstasy, while the lights of the chamber swam dim before his sight, and tears of pleasure trickled down his cheeks.

So the ninth hour passed; and they continued to converse, and to drink the cool purple wine, and to sing the songs of the years of Thang, until far into the night. More than once Ming-Y thought of departing; but each time Sie would begin, in that silver-sweet voice of hers, so wondrous a story of the great poets of the past, and of the women whom they loved, that he became as one entranced; or she would sing for him a song so strange that all his senses seemed to die except that of hearing. And at last, as she paused to pledge him in a cup of wine, Ming-Y could not restrain himself from putting his arm about her round neck and drawing her dainty head closer to him, and kissing the lips that were so much ruddier and sweeter than the wine. Then their lips separated no more – the night grew old, and they knew it not.

*   *   *

The birds awakened, the flowers opened their eyes to the rising sun, and Ming-Y found himself at last compelled to bid his lovely enchantress farewell. Sie, accompanying him to the terrace, kissed him fondly and said, 'Dear boy, come hither as often as you are able – as often as your heart whispers you to come. I know that you are not of those without faith and truth, who betray secrets; yet, being so young, you might also be sometimes thoughtless; and I pray you never to forget that only the stars have been the witnesses of our love. Speak of it to no living person, dearest; and take with you this little souvenir of our happy night.'

And she presented him with an exquisite and curious little thing – a paperweight in likeness of a couchant lion, wrought from a jade-stone yellow as that created by a rainbow in honour of Kong-fu-tze. Tenderly the boy kissed the gift and the beautiful hand that gave it. 'May the Spirits punish me,' he vowed, 'if ever I knowingly give you cause to reproach me, sweetheart!' And they separated with mutual vows.

That morning, on returning to the house of Lord Tchang, Ming-Y told the first falsehood which had ever passed his lips. He averred that his mother had requested him thenceforward to pass his nights at home, now that the weather had become so pleasant; for, though the way was somewhat long, he was strong and active, and needed both air and healthy exercise. Tchang believed all Ming-Y said, and offered no objection. Accordingly the lad found himself enabled to pass all his evenings at the house of the beautiful Sie. Each night they devoted to the same pleasures which had made their first acquaintance so charming: they sang and conversed by turns; they played at chess – the learned game invented by Wu-Wang, which is an imitation of war; they composed pieces of eighty rhymes upon the flowers, the trees, the clouds, the streams, the birds, the bees. But in all accomplishments Sie far excelled her young sweetheart. Whenever they played at chess, it was always Ming-Y's general, Ming-Y's *tsiang*, who was surrounded and vanquished; when they composed verses, Sie's poems were ever superior to his in harmony of word-colouring, in elegance of form, in classic loftiness of thought. And the themes they selected were always the most difficult – those of the poets of the Thang dynasty; the songs they sang were also the songs of five hundred years before – the songs of Youen-tchin, of Thou-mou, of Kao-pien above all, high poet and ruler of the province of Sze-tchouen.

So the summer waxed and waned upon their love, and the luminous autumn came, with its vapours of phantom gold, its shadows of magical purple.

*   *   *

Then it unexpectedly happened that the father of Ming-Y, meeting his son's employer at Tching-tou, was asked by him: 'Why must your boy continue to travel every evening to the city, now that the winter is approaching? The way is long, and when he returns in the morning he looks fordone with weariness. Why not permit him to slumber in my house during the season of snow?' And the father of Ming-Y, greatly astonished, responded: 'Sir, my son has not visited the city, nor has he been to our house all this summer. I fear that he must have acquired wicked habits, and that he passes his nights in evil company – perhaps in gaming, or in drinking with the women of the flower-boats.' But the High Commissioner returned: 'Nay! that is not to be thought of. I have never found any evil in the boy, and there are no taverns nor flower-boats nor any places of dissipation in our neighbourhood. No doubt Ming-Y has found some amiable youth of his own age with whom to spend his evenings, and only told me an untruth for fear that I would not otherwise permit him to leave my residence. I beg that you will say nothing to him until I shall have sought to discover this mystery; and this very evening I shall send my servant to follow after him, and to watch whither he goes.'

Pelou readily assented to this proposal, and promising to visit Tchang the following morning, returned to his home. In the evening, when Ming-Y left the house of Tchang, a servant followed him unobserved at a distance. But on reaching the most obscure portion of the road, the boy disappeared from sight as suddenly as though the earth had swallowed him. After having long sought after him in vain, the domestic returned in great bewilderment to the house, and related what had taken place. Tchang immediately sent a messenger to Pelou.

In the meantime Ming-Y, entering the chamber of his beloved, was surprised and deeply pained to find her in tears. 'Sweetheart,' she sobbed, wreathing her arms around his neck, 'we are about to be separated forever, because of reasons which I cannot tell you. From the very first I knew this must come to pass; and nevertheless it seemed to me for the moment so cruelly sudden a loss, so unexpected a misfortune, that I could not prevent myself from weeping! After this night we shall never see each other again, beloved, and I know that you will not be able to forget me while you live; but I know also that you will become a great scholar, and that honours and riches will be showered upon you, and that some beautiful and loving woman will console you for my loss. And now let us speak no more of grief; but let us pass this last evening joyously, so that your recollection of me may not be a painful one, and that you may remember my laughter rather than my tears.'

She brushed the bright drops away, and brought wine and music and the melodious *kin* of seven silken strings, and would not suffer Ming-Y to speak for one moment of the coming separation. And she sang him an ancient song about the calmness of summer lakes reflecting the blue of heaven only, and the calmness of the heart also, before the clouds of care and of grief and of weariness darken its little world. Soon they forgot their sorrow in the joy of song and wine; and those last hours seemed to Ming-Y more celestial than even the hours of their first bliss.

But when the yellow beauty of morning came their sadness returned, and they wept. Once more Sie accompanied her lover to the terrace-steps; and as she kissed him farewell, she pressed into his hand a parting gift – a little brush-case of agate, wonderfully chiselled, and worthy the table of a great poet. And they separated forever, shedding many tears.

*   *   *

Still Ming-Y could not believe it was an eternal parting. 'No!' he thought, 'I shall visit her tomorrow; for I cannot now live without her, and I feel assured that she cannot refuse to receive me.' Such were the thoughts that filled his mind as he reached the house of Tchang, to find his father and his patron standing on the porch awaiting him. Ere he could speak a word, Pelou demanded: 'Son, in what place have you been passing your nights?'

Seeing that his falsehood had been discovered, Ming-Y dared not make any reply, and remained abashed and silent, with bowed head, in the presence of his father. Then Pelou, striking the boy violently with his staff, commanded him to divulge the secret; and at last, partly through fear of his parent, and partly through fear of the law which ordains that '*the son refusing to obey his father shall be punished with one hundred blows of the bamboo*', Ming-Y faltered out the history of his love.

Tchang changed colour at the boy's tale. 'Child,' exclaimed the High Commissioner, 'I have no relative of the name of Ping; I have never heard of the woman you describe; I have never heard even of the house which you speak of. But I know also that you cannot dare to lie to Pelou, your honoured father; there is some strange delusion in all this affair.'

Then Ming-Y produced the gifts that Sie had given him – the lion of yellow jade, the brush-case of carven agate, also some original compositions made by the beautiful lady herself. The astonishment of Tchang was now shared by Pelou. Both observed that the brush-case of agate and the lion of jade bore the appearance of objects that had lain buried in the earth for centuries, and were of a workmanship beyond the power of living man to imitate; while the compositions proved to be veritable masterpieces of poetry, written in the style of the poets of the dynasty of Thang.

'Friend Pelou,' cried the High Commissioner, 'let us immediately accompany the boy to the place where he obtained these miraculous things, and apply the testimony of our senses to this mystery. The boy is no doubt telling the truth; yet his story passes my understanding.' And all three proceeded toward the place of the habitation of Sie.

*   *   *

But when they had arrived at the shadiest part of the road, where the perfumes were most sweet and the mosses were greenest, and the fruits of the wild peach flushed most pinkly, Ming-Y, gazing through the groves, uttered a cry of dismay. Where the azure-tiled roof had risen against the sky, there was now only the blue emptiness of air; where the green-and-gold façade had been, there was visible only the flickering of leaves under the aureate autumn light; and where the broad terrace had extended, could be discerned only a ruin – a tomb so ancient, so deeply gnawed by moss, that the name graven upon it was no longer decipherable. The home of Sie had disappeared!

All suddenly the High Commissioner smote his forehead with his hand, and turning to Pelou, recited the well-known verse of the ancient poet Tching-Kou: '*Surely the peach-flowers blossom over the tomb of SIE-THAO.*'

'Friend Pelou,' continued Tchang, 'the beauty who bewitched your son was no other than she whose tomb stands there in ruin before us! Did she not say she was wedded to Ping-Khang? There is no family of that name, but Ping-Khang is indeed the name of a broad alley in the city near. There was a dark riddle in all that she said. She called herself Sie of Moun-Hiao: there is no person of that name; there is no street of that name; but the Chinese characters *Moun* and *hiao*, placed together, form the character *Kiao*. Listen! The alley Ping-Khang, situated in the street Kiao, was the place where dwelt the great courtesans of the dynasty of Thang! Did she not sing the songs of Kao-pien? And upon the brush-case and the paperweight she gave your son, are there not characters which read, "Pure object of art belonging to Kao, of the city of Pho-hai"? That city no longer exists; but the memory of Kao-pien remains, for he was governor of the province of Sze-tchouen, and a mighty poet. And when he dwelt in the land of Chou, was not his favourite the beautiful wanton Sie – Sie-Thao, unmatched for grace among all the women of her day? It was he who made her a gift of those manuscripts of song; it was he who gave her those objects of rare art. Sie-Thao died not as other women die. Her limbs may have crumbled to dust; yet something of her still lives in this deep wood – her Shadow still haunts this shadowy place.'

Tchang ceased to speak. A vague fear fell upon the three. The thin mists of the morning made dim the distances of green, and deepened the ghostly beauty of the woods. A faint breeze passed by, leaving a trail of blossom-scent – a last odour of dying flowers – thin as that which clings to the silk of a forgotten robe; and, as it passed, the trees seemed to whisper across the silence, '*Sie-Thao*'.

* * *

Fearing greatly for his son, Pelou sent the lad away at once to the city of Kwang-tchau-fu. And there, in after years, Ming-Y obtained high dignities and honours by reason of his talents and his learning; and he married the daughter of an illustrious house, by whom he became the father of sons and daughters famous for their virtues and their accomplishments. Never could he forget Sie-Thao; and yet it is said that he never spoke of her – not even when his children begged him to tell them the story of two beautiful objects that always lay upon his writing-table: a lion of yellow jade, and a brush-case of carven agate.

THE LEGEND OF TCHI-NIU

A SOUND OF GONGS, A SOUND OF SONG —
THE SONG OF THE BUILDERS BUILDING
THE DWELLINGS OF THE DEAD

Khiu tchi ying-ying.
Tou tchi hoüng-hoüng.
Tcho tchi tong-tong.
Sio liu ping-ping.

The Legend of Tchi-Niu

In the quaint commentary accompanying the text of that holy book of Lao-tsu called *Kan-ing-p'ien* may be found a little story so old that the name of the one who first told it has been forgotten for a thousand years, yet so beautiful that it lives still in the memory of four hundred millions of people, like a prayer that, once learned, is forever remembered. The Chinese writer makes no mention of any city nor of any province, although even in the relation of the most ancient traditions such an omission is rare; we are only told that the name of the hero of the legend was Tong-yong, and that he lived in the years of the great dynasty of Han, some twenty centuries ago.

* * *

Tong-Yong's mother had died while he was yet an infant; and when he became a youth of nineteen years his father also passed away, leaving him utterly alone in the world, and without resources of any sort; for, being a very poor man, Tong's father had put himself to great straits to educate the lad, and had not been able to lay by even one copper coin of his earnings. And Tong lamented greatly to find himself so destitute that he could not honour the memory of that good father by having the customary rites of burial performed, and a carven tomb erected upon a propitious site. The poor only are friends of the poor; and among all those whom Tong knew, there was no-one able to assist him in defraying the expenses of the funeral. In one way only could the youth obtain money – by selling himself as a slave to some rich cultivator; and this he at last decided to do. In vain his friends did their utmost to dissuade him; and to no purpose did they attempt to delay the accomplishment of his sacrifice by beguiling promises of future aid. Tong only replied that he would sell his freedom a hundred times, if it were possible, rather than suffer his father's memory to remain unhonoured even for a brief season. And furthermore, confiding in his youth and strength, he determined to put a high price upon his servitude – a price which would enable him to build a handsome tomb, but which it would be well-nigh impossible for him ever to repay.

*   *   *

Accordingly he repaired to the broad public place where slaves and debtors were exposed for sale, and seated himself upon a bench of stone, having affixed to his shoulders a placard inscribed with the terms of his servitude and the list of his qualifications as a labourer. Many who read the characters upon the placard smiled disdainfully at the price asked, and passed on without a word; others lingered only to question him out of simple curiosity; some commended him with hollow praise; some openly mocked his unselfishness, and laughed at his childish piety. Thus many hours wearily passed, and Tong had almost despaired of finding a master, when there rode up a high official of the province – a grave and handsome man, lord of a thousand slaves, and owner of vast estates. Reining in his Tartar horse, the official halted to read the placard and to consider the value of the slave. He did not smile, or advise, or ask any questions; but having observed the price asked, and the fine strong limbs of the youth, purchased him without further ado, merely ordering his attendant to pay the sum and to see that the necessary papers were made out.

*   *   *

Thus Tong found himself enabled to fulfil the wish of his heart, and to have a monument built which, although of small size, was destined to delight the eyes of all who beheld it, being designed by cunning artists and executed by skilful sculptors. And while it was yet designed only, the pious rites were performed, the silver coin was placed in the mouth of the dead, the white lanterns were hung at the door, the holy prayers were recited, and paper shapes of all things the departed might need in the land of the Genii were consumed in consecrated fire. And after the geomancers and the necromancers had chosen a burial-spot which no unlucky star could shine upon, a place of rest which no demon or dragon might ever disturb, the beautiful *chih* was built. Then was the phantom money strewn along the way; the funeral procession departed from the dwelling of the dead, and with prayers and lamentation the mortal remains of Tong's good father were borne to the tomb.

Then Tong entered as a slave into the service of his purchaser, who allotted him a little hut to dwell in; and thither Tong carried with him those wooden tablets, bearing the ancestral names, before which filial piety must daily burn the incense of prayer, and perform the tender duties of family worship.

* * *

Thrice had spring perfumed the breast of the land with flowers, and thrice had been celebrated that festival of the dead which is called *Siu-fan-ti*, and thrice had Tong swept and garnished his father's tomb and presented his fivefold offering of fruits and meats. The period of mourning had passed, yet he had not ceased to mourn for his parent. The years revolved with their moons, bringing him no hour of joy, no day of happy rest; yet he never lamented his servitude, or failed to perform the rites of ancestral worship – until at last the fever of the rice-fields laid strong hold upon him, and he could not arise from his couch; and his fellow-labourers thought him destined to die. There was no-one to wait upon him, no-one to care for his needs, inasmuch as slaves and servants were wholly busied with the duties of the household or the labour of the fields – all departing to toil at sunrise and returning weary only after the sundown.

Now, while the sick youth slumbered the fitful slumber of exhaustion one sultry noon, he dreamed that a strange and beautiful woman stood by him, and bent above him and touched his forehead with the long, fine fingers of her shapely hand. And at her cool touch a weird sweet shock passed through him, and all his veins tingled as if thrilled by new life. Opening his eyes in wonder, he saw verily bending over him the charming being of whom he had dreamed, and he knew that her lithe hand really caressed his throbbing forehead. But the flame of the fever was gone, a delicious coolness now penetrated every fibre of his body, and the thrill of which he had dreamed still tingled in his blood like a great joy. Even at the same moment the eyes of the gentle visitor met his own, and he saw they were singularly beautiful, and shone like splendid black jewels under brows curved like the wings of the swallow. Yet their calm gaze seemed to pass through him as light through crystal; and a vague awe came upon him, so that the question which had risen to his lips found no utterance. Then she, still caressing him, smiled and said: 'I have come to restore thy strength and to be thy wife. Arise and worship with me.'

Her clear voice had tones melodious as a bird's song; but in her gaze there was an imperious power which Tong felt he dare not resist. Rising from his couch, he was astounded to find his strength wholly restored; but the cool, slender hand which held his own led him away so swiftly that he had little time for amazement. He would have given years of existence for courage to speak of his misery, to declare his utter inability to maintain a wife; but something irresistible in the long dark eyes of his companion forbade him to speak; and as though his inmost thought had been discerned by that wondrous gaze, she said to him, in the same clear voice, '*I will provide.*' Then shame made him blush at the thought of his wretched aspect and tattered apparel; but he observed that she also was poorly attired, like a woman of the people – wearing no ornament of any sort, nor even shoes upon her feet. And before he had yet spoken to her, they came before the ancestral tablets; and there she knelt with him and prayed, and pledged him in a cup of wine – brought he knew not from whence – and together they worshipped Heaven and Earth. Thus she became his wife.

*   *   *

A mysterious marriage it seemed, for neither on that day nor at any future time could Tong venture to ask his wife the name of her family, or of the place whence she came, and he could not answer any of the curious questions which his fellow-labourers put to him concerning her; and she, moreover, never uttered a word about herself, except to say that her name was Tchi. But although Tong had such awe of her that while her eyes were upon him he was as one having no will of his own, he loved her unspeakably; and the thought of his serfdom ceased to weigh upon him from the hour of his marriage. As through magic the little dwelling had become transformed: its misery was masked with charming paper devices – with dainty decorations created out of nothing by that pretty jugglery of which woman only knows the secret.

Each morning at dawn the young husband found a well-prepared and ample repast awaiting him, and each evening also upon his return; but the wife all day sat at her loom, weaving silk after a fashion unlike anything which had ever been seen before in that province. For as she wove, the silk flowed from the loom like a slow current of glossy gold, bearing upon its undulations strange forms of violet and crimson and jewel-green: shapes of ghostly horsemen riding upon horses, and of phantom chariots dragon-drawn, and of standards of trailing cloud. In every dragon's beard glimmered the mystic pearl; in every rider's helmet sparkled the gem of rank. And each day Tchi would weave a great piece of such figured silk; and the fame of her weaving spread abroad. From far and near people thronged to see the marvellous work; and the silk-merchants of great cities heard of it, and they sent messengers to Tchi, asking her that she should weave for them and teach them her secret. Then she wove for them, as they desired, in return for the silver cubes which they brought her; but when they prayed her to teach them, she laughed and said, 'Assuredly I could never teach you, for no-one among you has fingers like mine.' And indeed no man could discern her fingers when she wove, any more than he might behold the wings of a bee vibrating in swift flight.

* * *

The seasons passed, and Tong never knew want, so well did his beautiful wife fulfil her promise – '*I will provide*'; and the cubes of bright silver brought by the silk-merchants were piled up higher and higher in the great carven chest which Tchi had bought for the storage of the household goods.

One morning, at last, when Tong, having finished his repast, was about to depart to the fields, Tchi unexpectedly bade him remain; and opening the great chest, she took out of it and gave him a document written in the official characters called *li-shu*. And Tong, looking at it, cried out and leaped in his joy, for it was the certificate of his manumission. Tchi had secretly purchased her husband's freedom with the price of her wondrous silks!

'Thou shalt labour no more for any master,' she said, 'but for thine own sake only. And I have also bought this dwelling, with all which is therein, and the tea-fields to the south, and the mulberry groves hard by – all of which are thine.'

Then Tong, beside himself for gratefulness, would have prostrated himself in worship before her, but that she would not suffer it.

* * *

Thus he was made free; and prosperity came to him with his freedom; and whatsoever he gave to the sacred earth was returned to him centupled; and his servants loved him and blessed the beautiful Tchi, so silent and yet so kindly to all about her. But the silk-loom soon remained untouched, for Tchi gave birth to a son – a boy so beautiful that Tong wept with delight when he looked upon him. And thereafter the wife devoted herself wholly to the care of the child.

Now it soon became manifest that the boy was not less wonderful than his wonderful mother. In the third month of his age he could speak; in the seventh month he could repeat by heart the proverbs of the sages, and recite the holy prayers; before the eleventh month he could use the writing-brush with skill, and copy in shapely characters the precepts of Lao-tsu. And the priests of the temples came to behold him and to converse with him, and they marvelled at the charm of the child and the wisdom of what he said; and they blessed Tong, saying: 'Surely this son of thine is a gift from the Master of Heaven, a sign that the immortals love thee. May thine eyes behold a hundred happy summers!'

*   *   *

It was in the Period of the Eleventh Moon: the flowers had passed away, the perfume of the summer had flown, the winds were growing chill, and in Tong's home the evening fires were lighted. Long the husband and wife sat in the mellow glow – he speaking much of his hopes and joys, and of his son that was to be so grand a man, and of many paternal projects; while she, speaking little, listened to his words, and often turned her wonderful eyes upon him with an answering smile. Never had she seemed so beautiful before; and Tong, watching her face, marked not how the night waned, nor how the fire sank low, nor how the wind sang in the leafless trees without.

All suddenly Tchi arose without speaking, and took his hand in hers and led him, gently as on that strange wedding-morning, to the cradle where their boy slumbered, faintly smiling in his dreams. And in that moment there came upon Tong the same strange fear that he knew when Tchi's eyes had first met his own – the vague fear that love and trust had calmed, but never wholly cast out, like unto the fear of the gods. And all unknowingly, like one yielding to the pressure of mighty invisible hands, he bowed himself low before her, kneeling as to a divinity. Now, when he lifted his eyes again to her face, he closed them forthwith in awe; for she towered before him taller than any mortal woman, and there was a glow about her as of sunbeams, and the light of her limbs shone through her garments. But her sweet voice came to him with all the tenderness of other hours, saying: 'Lo! my beloved, the moment has come in which I must forsake thee; for I was never of mortal born, and the Invisible may incarnate themselves for a time only. Yet I leave with thee the pledge of our love – this fair son, who shall ever be to thee as faithful and as fond as thou thyself hast been. Know, my beloved, that I was sent to thee even by the Master of Heaven, in reward of thy filial piety, and that I must now return to the glory of His house: *I am the goddess Tchi-Niu.*'

Even as she ceased to speak, the great glow faded; and Tong, reopening his eyes, knew that she had passed away forever – mysteriously as pass the winds of heaven, irrevocably as the light of a flame blown out. Yet all the doors were barred, all the windows unopened. Still the child slept, smiling in his sleep. Outside, the darkness was breaking; the sky was brightening swiftly; the night was past. With splendid majesty the East threw open high gates of gold for the coming of the sun; and, illuminated by the glory of his coming, the vapours of morning wrought themselves into marvellous shapes of shifting colour – into forms weirdly beautiful as the silken dreams woven in the loom of Tchi-Niu.

THE RETURN OF YEN-TCHIN-KING

Before me ran, as a herald runneth,
the Leader of the Moon;
And the Spirit of the Wind followed after me –
quickening his flight.

LI–SAO

The Return of Yen-Tchin-King

In the thirty-eighth chapter of the holy book *Kan-ing-p'ien*, wherein the Recompense of Immortality is considered, may be found the legend of Yen-Tchin-King. A thousand years have passed since the passing of the good Tchin-King; for it was in the period of the greatness of Thang that he lived and died.

Now, in those days when Yen-Tchin-King was Supreme Judge of one of the Six August Tribunals, one Li-hi-lie, a soldier mighty for evil, lifted the black banner of revolt, and drew after him, as a tide of destruction, the millions of the northern provinces. And learning of these things, and knowing also that Hi-lie was the most ferocious of men, who respected nothing on earth save fearlessness, the Son of Heaven commanded Tchin-King that he should visit Hi-lie and strive to recall the rebel to duty, and read unto the people who followed after him in revolt the Emperor's letter of reproof and warning. For Tchin-King was famed throughout the provinces for his wisdom, his rectitude, and his fearlessness; and the Son of Heaven believed that if Hi-lie would listen to the words of any living man steadfast in loyalty and virtue, he would listen to the words of Tchin-King. So Tchin-King arrayed himself in his robes of office, and set his house in order; and, having embraced his wife and his children, mounted his horse and rode away alone to the roaring camp of the rebels, bearing the Emperor's letter in his bosom. 'I shall return; fear not!' were his last words to the grey servant who watched him from the terrace as he rode.

* * *

And Tchin-King at last descended from his horse, and entered into the rebel camp, and, passing through that huge gathering of war, stood in the presence of Hi-lie. High sat the rebel among his chiefs, encircled by the wave-lightning of swords and the thunders of ten thousand gongs: above him undulated the silken folds of the Black Dragon, while a vast fire rose bickering before him. Also Tchin-King saw that the tongues of that fire were licking human bones, and that skulls of men lay blackening among the ashes. Yet he was not afraid to look upon the fire, nor into the eyes of Hi-lie; but drawing from his bosom the roll of perfumed yellow silk upon which the words of the Emperor were written, and kissing it, he made ready to read, while the multitude became silent. Then, in a strong, clear voice he began: '*The words of the Celestial and August, the Son of Heaven, the Divine Ko-Tsu-Tchin-Yao-ti, unto the rebel Li-Hi-lie and those that follow him.*'

And a roar went up like the roar of the sea – a roar of rage, and the hideous battle-moan, like the moan of a forest in storm – 'Hoo! Hoo-oo-oo-oo!' – and the sword-lightnings brake loose, and the thunder of the gongs moved the ground beneath the messenger's feet. But Hi-lie waved his gilded wand, and again there was silence. 'Nay!' spake the rebel chief; 'let the dog bark!' So Tchin-King spake on: '*Knowest thou not, O most rash and foolish of men, that thou leadest the people only into the mouth of the Dragon of Destruction? Knowest thou not, also, that the people of my kingdom are the first-born of the Master of Heaven? So it hath been written that he who doth needlessly subject the people to wounds and death shall not be suffered by Heaven to live! Thou who wouldst subvert those laws founded by the wise – those laws in obedience to which may happiness and prosperity alone be found – thou art committing the greatest of all crimes – the crime that is never forgiven!*

'*O my people, think not that I your Emperor, I your Father, seek your destruction. I desire only your happiness, your prosperity, your greatness; let not your folly provoke the severity of your Celestial Parent. Follow not after madness and blind rage; hearken rather to the wise words of my messenger.*'

'Hoo! hoo-oo-oo-oo-oo!' roared the people, gathering fury. 'Hoo! hoo-oo-oo-oo!' – till the mountains rolled back the cry like the rolling of a typhoon; and once more the pealing of the gongs paralysed voice and hearing. Then Tchin-King, looking at Hi-lie, saw that he laughed, and that the words of the letter would not again be listened to. Therefore he read on to the end without looking about him, resolved to perform his mission in so far as lay in his power. And having read all, he would have given the letter to Hi-lie; but Hi-lie would not extend his hand to take it. Therefore Tchin-King replaced it in his bosom, and folding his arms, looked Hi-lie calmly in the face, and waited. Again Hi-lie waved his gilded wand; and the roaring ceased, and the booming of the gongs, until nothing save the fluttering of the Dragon-banner could be heard. Then spake Hi-lie, with an evil smile: 'Tchin-King, O son of a dog! if thou dost not now take the oath of fealty, and bow thyself before me, and salute me with the salutation of Emperors – even with the *luh-kao*, the triple prostration – into that fire thou shalt be thrown.'

But Tchin-King, turning his back upon the usurper, bowed himself a moment in worship to Heaven and Earth; and then rising suddenly, ere any man could lay hand upon him, he leaped into the towering flame, and stood there, with folded arms, like a god.

Then Hi-lie leaped to his feet in amazement, and shouted to his men; and they snatched Tchin-King from the fire, and wrung the flames from his robes with their naked hands, and extolled him, and praised him to his face. And even Hi-lie himself descended from his seat, and spoke fair words to him, saying: 'O Tchin-King, I see thou art indeed a brave man and true, and worthy of all honour; be seated among us, I pray thee, and partake of whatever it is in our power to bestow!'

But Tchin-King, looking upon him unswervingly, replied in a voice clear as the voice of a great bell: 'Never, O Hi-lie, shall I accept aught from thy hand, save death, so long as thou shalt continue in the path of wrath and folly. And never shall it be said that Tchin-King sat him down among rebels and traitors, among murderers and robbers.'

Then Hi-lie in sudden fury, smote him with his sword; and Tchin-King fell to the earth and died, striving even in his death to bow his head toward the South – toward the place of the Emperor's palace – toward the presence of his beloved Master.

* * *

Even at the same hour the Son of Heaven, alone in the inner chamber of his palace, became aware of a Shape prostrate before his feet; and when he spake, the Shape arose and stood before him, and he saw that it was Tchin-King. And the Emperor would have questioned him; yet ere he could question, the familiar voice spake, saying: 'Son of Heaven, the mission confided to me I have performed; and thy command hath been accomplished to the extent of thy humble servant's feeble power. But even now must I depart, that I may enter the service of another Master.'

And looking, the Emperor perceived that the Golden Tigers upon the wall were visible through the form of Tchin-King; and a strange coldness, like a winter wind, passed through the chamber;

and the figure faded out. Then the Emperor knew that the Master of whom his faithful servant had spoken was none other than the Master of Heaven.

Also at the same hour the grey servant of Tchin-King's house beheld him passing through the apartments, smiling as he was wont to smile when he saw that all things were as he desired. 'Is it well with thee, my lord?' questioned the aged man. And a voice answered him: 'It is well'; but the presence of Tchin-King had passed away before the answer came.

*   *   *

So the armies of the Son of Heaven strove with the rebels. But the land was soaked with blood and blackened with fire; and the corpses of whole populations were carried by the rivers to feed the fishes of the sea; and still the war prevailed through many a long red year. Then came to aid the Son of Heaven the hordes that dwell in the desolations of the West and North – horsemen born, a nation of wild archers, each mighty to bend a two-hundred-pound bow until the ears should meet. And as a whirlwind they came against rebellion, raining raven-feathered arrows in a storm of death; and they prevailed against Hi-lie and his people. Then those that survived destruction and defeat submitted, and promised allegiance; and once more was the law of righteousness restored. But Tchin-King had been dead for many summers.

And the Son of Heaven sent word to his victorious generals that they should bring back with them the bones of his faithful servant, to be laid with honour in a mausoleum erected by imperial decree. So the generals of the Celestial and August sought after the nameless grave and found it, and had the earth taken up, and made ready to remove the coffin.

But the coffin crumbled into dust before their eyes; for the worms had gnawed it, and the hungry earth had devoured its substance, leaving only a phantom shell that vanished at touch of the light. And lo! as it vanished, all beheld lying there the perfect form and features of the good Tchin-King. Corruption had not touched him, nor had the worms disturbed his rest, nor had the bloom of life departed from his face. And he seemed to dream only – comely to see as upon the morning of his bridal, and smiling as the holy images smile, with eyelids closed, in the twilight of the great pagodas.

Then spoke a priest, standing by the grave: 'O my children, this is indeed a Sign from the Master of Heaven; in such wise do the

Powers Celestial preserve them that are chosen to be numbered with the Immortals. Death may not prevail over them, neither may corruption come nigh them. Verily the blessed Tchin-King hath taken his place among the divinities of Heaven!'

Then they bore Tchin-King back to his native place, and laid him with highest honours in the mausoleum which the Emperor had commanded; and there he sleeps, incorruptible forever, arrayed in his robes of state. Upon his tomb are sculptured the emblems of his greatness and his wisdom and his virtue, and the signs of his office, and the Four Precious Things: and the monsters which are holy symbols mount giant guard in stone about it; and the weird Dogs of Fo keep watch before it, as before the temples of the gods.

THE TRADITION OF THE TEA-PLANT

SANG A CHINESE HEART FOURTEEN
HUNDRED YEARS AGO

There is Somebody of whom I am thinking.
Far away there is Somebody of whom I am thinking.
A hundred leagues of mountains lie between us –
Yet the same Moon shines upon us, and the passing Wind
  breathes upon us both.

The Tradition of the Tea-Plant

Good is the continence of the eye;
Good is the continence of the ear;
Good is the continence of the nostrils;
Good is the continence of the tongue;
Good is the continence of the body;
Good is the continence of speech;
Good is all . . .

Again the Vulture of Temptation soared to the highest heaven of his
contemplation, bringing his soul down, down, reeling and fluttering,
back to the World of Illusion. Again the memory made dizzy his
thought, like the perfume of some venomous flower. Yet he had seen
the bayadere for an instant only, when passing through Kasi upon his
way to China – to the vast empire of souls that thirsted after the
refreshment of Buddha's law, as sun-parched fields thirst for the life-
giving rain. When she called him, and dropped her little gift into his
mendicant's bowl, he had indeed lifted his fan before his face, yet not
quickly enough; and the penalty of that fault had followed him a
thousand leagues – pursued after him even into the strange land to
which he had come to hear the words of the Universal Teacher.
Accursed beauty! Surely framed by the Tempter of tempters, by
Mara himself, for the perdition of the just! Wisely had Bhagavat
warned his disciples: 'O ye Cramanas, women are not to be looked
upon! And if ye chance to meet women, ye must not suffer your eyes
to dwell upon them; but, maintaining holy reserve, speak not to
them at all. Then fail not to whisper unto your own hearts, "Lo, we
are Cramanas, whose duty it is to remain uncontaminated by the
corruptions of this world, even as the Lotos, which suffereth no
vileness to cling unto its leaves, though it blossom amid the refuse of
the wayside ditch." ' Then also came to his memory, but with a new
and terrible meaning, the words of the Twentieth-and-Third of
the Admonitions: 'Of all attachments unto objects of desire, the
strongest indeed is the attachment to form. Happily, this passion is

unique; for were there any other like unto it, then to enter the Perfect Way were impossible.'

How, indeed, thus haunted by the illusion of form, was he to fulfil the vow that he had made to pass a night and a day in perfect and unbroken meditation? Already the night was beginning! Assuredly, for sickness of the soul, for fever of the spirit, there was no physic save prayer. The sunset was swiftly fading out. He strove to pray.

'*O the Jewel in the Lotos!*

'Even as the tortoise withdraweth its extremities into its shell, let me, O Blessed One, withdraw my senses wholly into meditation!

'*O the Jewel in the Lotos!*

'For even as rain penetrateth the broken roof of a dwelling long uninhabited, so may passion enter the soul uninhabited by meditation.

'*O the Jewel in the Lotos!*

'Even as still water that hath deposited all its slime, so let my soul, O Tathagata, be made pure! Give me strong power to rise above the world, O Master, even as the wild bird rises from its marsh to follow the pathway of the Sun!

'*O the Jewel in the Lotos!*

'By day shineth the sun, by night shineth the moon; shineth also the warrior in harness of war; shineth likewise in meditations the Cramana. But the Buddha at all times, by night or by day, shineth ever the same, illuminating the world.

'*O the Jewel in the Lotos!*

'Let me cease, O thou Perfectly Awakened, to remain as an Ape in the World-forest, forever ascending and descending in search of the fruits of folly. Swift as the twining of serpents, vast as the growth of lianas in a forest, are the all-encircling growths of the Plant of Desire.

'*O the Jewel in the Lotos!*

Vain his prayer, alas! Vain also his invocation! The mystic meaning of the holy text – the sense of the Lotos, the sense of the Jewel – had evaporated from the words, and their monotonous utterance now served only to lend more dangerous definition to the memory that tempted and tortured him. *O the jewel in her ear!* What lotos-bud more dainty than the folded flower of flesh, with its dripping of diamond-fire! Again he saw it, and the curve of the cheek beyond, luscious to look upon as beautiful brown fruit. How true the Two Hundred and Eighty-Fourth verse of the Admonitions! – 'So long as a man shall not have torn from his heart even the smallest rootlet of that liana of desire which draweth his thought toward women, even so long shall his soul remain fettered.' And there came to his mind also the Three Hundred and Forty-Fifth verse of the same blessed book, regarding fetters.

'In bonds of rope, wise teachers have said, there is no strength; nor in fetters of wood, nor yet in fetters of iron. Much stronger than any of these is the fetter of *concern for the jewelled earrings of women.*'

'Omniscient Gotama!' he cried – 'all-seeing Tathagata! How multiform the Consolation of Thy Word! How marvellous Thy understanding of the human heart! Was this also one of Thy temptations? – One of the myriad illusions marshalled before Thee by Mara in that night when the earth rocked as a chariot, and the sacred trembling passed from sun to sun, from system to system, from universe to universe, from eternity to eternity?'

O the jewel in her ear! The vision would not go! Nay, each time it hovered before his thought it seemed to take a warmer life, a fonder look, a fairer form; to develop with his weakness; to gain force from his enervation. He saw the eyes, large, limpid, soft, and black as a deer's; the pearls in the dark hair, and the pearls in the pink mouth; the lips curling to a kiss, a flower-kiss; and a fragrance seemed to float to his senses, sweet, strange, soporific – a perfume of youth, an odour of woman. Rising to his feet, with strong resolve he pronounced again the sacred invocation; and he recited the holy words of the *Chapter of Impermanency*:

'Gazing upon the heavens and upon the earth ye must say, *These are not permanent*. Gazing upon the mountains and the rivers, ye must say, *These are not permanent*. Gazing upon the forms and upon the faces of exterior beings, and beholding their growth and their development, ye must say, *These are not permanent.*'

And nevertheless! how sweet illusion! The illusion of the great sun; the illusion of the shadow-casting hills; the illusion of waters, formless and multiform; the illusion of – nay, nay! what impious fancy! Accursed girl! Yet, yet! why should he curse her? Had she ever done aught to merit the malediction of an ascetic? Never, never! Only her form, the memory of her, the beautiful phantom of her, the accursed phantom of her! What was she? An illusion creating illusions, a mockery, a dream, a shadow, a vanity, a vexation of spirit! The fault, the sin, was in himself, in his rebellious thought, in his untamed memory. Though mobile as water, intangible as vapour, Thought, nevertheless, may be tamed by the Will, may be harnessed to the chariot of Wisdom – must be! – that happiness be found. And he recited the blessed verses of the 'Book of the Way of the Law':

'*All forms are only temporary*.' When this great truth is fully comprehended by anyone, then is he delivered from all pain. This is the Way of Purification.

'*All forms are subject unto pain*.' When this great truth is fully comprehended by anyone, then is he delivered from all pain. This is the Way of Purification.

'*All forms are without substantial reality*.' When this great truth is fully comprehended by anyone, then is he delivered from all pain. This is the way of . . .

Her form, too, unsubstantial, unreal, an illusion only, though comeliest of illusions? She had given him alms! Was the merit of the giver illusive also – illusive like the grace of the supple fingers that gave? Assuredly there were mysteries in the Abhidharma impenetrable, incomprehensible! . . . It was a golden coin, stamped with the symbol of an elephant – not more of an illusion, indeed, than the gifts of Kings to the Buddha! Gold upon her bosom also, less fine than the gold of her skin. Naked between the silken sash and the narrow breast-corselet, her young waist curved glossy and pliant as a bow. Richer the silver in her voice than in the hollow *pagals* that made a moonlight about her ankles! But her smile! – the little teeth like flower-stamens in the perfumed blossom of her mouth!

O weakness! O shame! How had the strong Charioteer of Resolve thus lost his control over the wild team of fancy! Was this languor of the Will a signal of coming peril, the peril of slumber? So strangely vivid those fancies were, so brightly definite, as about to take visible form, to move with factitious life, to play some unholy drama upon the stage of dreams! 'O Thou Fully Awakened!' he cried aloud, 'help now thy humble disciple to obtain the blessed wakefulness of perfect contemplation! Let him find force to fulfil his vow! Suffer not Mara to prevail against him!' And he recited the eternal verses of the Chapter of Wakefulness: '*Completely and eternally awake are the disciples of Gotama!* Unceasingly, by day and night, their thoughts are fixed upon the Law.

'*Completely and eternally awake are the disciples of Gotama!* Unceasingly, by day and night, their thoughts are fixed upon the Community.

'*Completely and eternally awake are the disciples of Gotama!* Unceasingly, by day and night, their thoughts are fixed upon the Body.

'*Completely and eternally awake are the disciples of Gotama!* Unceasingly, by day and night, their minds know the sweetness of perfect peace.

'*Completely and eternally awake are the disciples of Gotama!* Unceasingly, by day and night, their minds enjoy the deep peace of meditation.'

There came a murmur to his ears; a murmuring of many voices, smothering the utterances of his own, like a tumult of waters. The stars went out before his sight; the heavens darkened their infinities: all things became viewless, became blackness; and the great murmur deepened, like the murmur of a rising tide; and the earth seemed to sink from beneath him. His feet no longer touched the ground; a sense of supernatural buoyancy pervaded every fibre of his body: he felt himself floating in obscurity; then sinking softly, slowly, like a feather dropped from the pinnacle of a temple. Was this death? Nay, for all suddenly, as transported by the Sixth Supernatural Power, he stood again in light – a perfumed, sleepy light, vapoury, beautiful – that bathed the marvellous streets of some Indian city. Now the nature of the murmur became manifest to him; for he moved with a mighty throng, a people of pilgrims, a nation of worshippers. But these were not of his faith; they bore upon their foreheads the smeared symbols of obscene gods! Still, he could not escape from their midst; the mile-broad human torrent bore him irresistibly with it, as a leaf is swept by the waters of the Ganges. Rajahs were there with their trains, and princes riding upon elephants, and Brahmins robed in their vestments, and swarms of voluptuous dancing-girls, moving to chant of *kabit* and *damari*. But whither, whither? Out of the city into the sun they passed, between avenues of banyan, down colonnades of palm. But whither, whither?

Blue-distant, a mountain of carven stone appeared before them – the Temple, lifting to heaven its wilderness of chiselled pinnacles, flinging to the sky the golden spray of its decoration. Higher it grew with approach, the blue tones changed to grey, the outlines sharpened in the light. Then each detail became visible: the elephants of the pedestals standing upon tortoises of rock; the great grim faces of the capitals; the serpents and monsters writhing among the friezes; the many-headed gods of basalt in their galleries of fretted niches, tier above tier; the pictured foulnesses, the painted lusts, the divinities of abomination. And, yawning in the sloping precipice of sculpture, beneath a frenzied swarming of gods and Gopia – a beetling pyramid of limbs and bodies interlocked – the Gate, cavernous and shadowy as the mouth of Siva, devoured the living multitude.

The eddy of the throng whirled him with it to the vastness of the interior. None seemed to note his yellow robe, none even to observe his presence. Giant aisles intercrossed their heights above him; myriads of mighty pillars, fantastically carven, filed away to invisibility behind the yellow illumination of torch-fires. Strange images, weirdly sensuous, loomed up through haze of incense. Colossal figures, that at a distance assumed the form of elephants or garuda-birds, changed aspect when approached, and revealed as the secret of their design an interplaiting of the bodies of women; while one divinity rode all the monstrous allegories – one divinity or demon, eternally the same in the repetition of the sculptor, universally visible as though self-multiplied. The huge pillars themselves were symbols, figures, carnalities; the orgiastic spirit of that worship lived and writhed in the contorted bronze of the lamps, the twisted gold of the cups, the chiselled marble of the tanks . . .

How far had he proceeded? He knew not; the journey among those countless columns, past those armies of petrified gods, down lanes of flickering lights, seemed longer than the voyage of a caravan, longer than his pilgrimage to China! But suddenly, inexplicably, there came a silence as of cemeteries; the living ocean seemed to have ebbed away from about him, to have been engulfed within abysses of subterranean architecture! He found himself alone in some strange crypt before a basin, shell-shaped and shallow, bearing in its centre a rounded column of less than human height, whose smooth and spherical summit was wreathed with flowers. Lamps similarly formed, and fed with oil of palm, hung above it. There was no other graven image, no visible divinity. Flowers of countless varieties lay heaped upon the pavement; they covered its surface like a carpet, thick, soft; they exhaled their ghosts beneath his feet. The perfume seemed to penetrate his brain – a perfume sensuous, intoxicating, unholy; an unconquerable languor mastered his will, and he sank to rest upon the floral offerings.

The sound of a tread, light as a whisper, approached through the heavy stillness, with a drowsy tinkling of *pagals*, a tintinnabulation of anklets. All suddenly he felt glide about his neck the tepid smoothness of a woman's arm. *She, she!* His Illusion, his Temptation; but how transformed, transfigured! – Preternatural in her loveliness, incomprehensible in her charm! Delicate as a jasmine-petal the cheek that touched his own; deep as night, sweet as summer, the eyes that watched him. '*Heart's-thief*,' her flower-lips whispered – '*Heart's-thief, how have I sought for thee! How have I found thee! Sweets I bring thee, my beloved; lips and bosom; fruit and blossom. Hast thirst? Drink from the well of mine eyes! Wouldst sacrifice? I am thine altar! Wouldst pray? I am thy God!'*

Their lips touched; her kiss seemed to change the cells of his blood to flame. For a moment Illusion triumphed; Mara prevailed! . . . With a shock of resolve the dreamer awoke in the night – under the stars of the Chinese sky.

Only a mockery of sleep! But the vow had been violated, the sacred purpose unfulfilled! Humiliated, penitent, but resolved, the ascetic drew from his girdle a keen knife, and with unfaltering hands severed his eyelids from his eyes, and flung them from him. 'O Thou Perfectly Awakened!' he prayed, 'thy disciple hath not been overcome save through the feebleness of the body; and his vow hath been renewed. Here shall he linger, without food or drink, until the moment of its fulfilment.' And having assumed the hieratic posture – seated himself with his lower limbs folded beneath him, and the palms of his hands upward, the right upon the left, the left resting upon the sole of his upturned foot – he resumed his meditation.

*   *   *

Dawn blushed; day brightened. The sun shortened all the shadows of the land, and lengthened them again, and sank at last upon his funeral pyre of crimson-burning cloud. Night came and glittered and passed. But Mara had tempted in vain. This time the vow had been fulfilled, the holy purpose accomplished.

And again the sun arose to fill the world with laughter of light; flowers opened their hearts to him; birds sang their morning hymn of fire-worship; the deep forest trembled with delight; and far upon the plain, the eaves of many-storeyed temples and the peaked caps of the city-towers caught aureate glory. Strong in the holiness of his accomplished vow, the Indian pilgrim arose in the morning glow. He started for amazement as he lifted his hands to his eyes. What! Was everything a dream? Impossible! Yet now his eyes felt no pain; neither were they lidless; not even so much as one of their lashes was lacking. What marvel had been wrought? In vain he looked for the severed lids that he had flung upon the ground; they had mysteriously vanished. But lo! There where he had cast them two wondrous shrubs were growing, with dainty leaflets eyelid-shaped, and snowy buds just opening to the East.

Then, by virtue of the supernatural power acquired in that mighty meditation, it was given the holy missionary to know the secret of that newly created plant – the subtle virtue of its leaves. And he named it, in the language of the nation to whom he brought the Lotos of the Good Law, '*TE*'; and he spake to it, saying: 'Blessed be thou, sweet plant, beneficent, life-giving, formed by the spirit of virtuous resolve! Lo! the fame of thee shall yet spread unto the ends of the earth; and the perfume of thy life be borne unto the uttermost parts by all the winds of heaven! Verily, for all time to come men who drink of thy sap shall find such refreshment that weariness may not overcome them nor languor seize upon them – neither shall they know the confusion of drowsiness, nor any desire for slumber in the hour of duty or of prayer. Blessed be thou!'

*   *   *

And still, as a mist of incense, as a smoke of universal sacrifice, perpetually ascends to heaven from all the lands of earth the pleasant vapour of TE, created for the refreshment of mankind by the power of a holy vow, the virtue of a pious atonement.

THE TALE OF THE PORCELAIN-GOD

It is written in the Fong-ho-chin-tch'ouen, *that whenever the artist Thsang-Kong was in doubt, he would look into the fire of the great oven in which his vases were baking, and question the Guardian-Spirit dwelling in the flame. And the Spirit of the Oven-fires so aided him with his counsels, that the porcelains made by Thsang-Kong were indeed finer and lovelier to look upon than all other porcelains. And they were baked in the years of Khang-hi — sacredly called Jin Houang-ti.*

The Tale of the Porcelain-God

Who first of men discovered the secret of the *Kao-ling*, of the *Pe-tun-tse* – the bones and the flesh, the skeleton and the skin, of the beauteous Vase? Who first discovered the virtue of the curd-white clay? Who first prepared the ice-pure bricks of *tun*: the gathered-hoariness of mountains that have died for age; blanched dust of the rocky bones and the stony flesh of sun-seeking Giants that have ceased to be? Unto whom was it first given to discover the divine art of porcelain?

Unto Pu, once a man, now a god, before whose snowy statues bow the myriad populations enrolled in the guilds of the potteries. But the place of his birth we know not; perhaps the tradition of it may have been effaced from remembrance by that awful war which in our own day consumed the lives of twenty millions of the Black-haired Race, and obliterated from the face of the world even the wonderful City of Porcelain itself – the City of King-te-chin, that of old shone like a jewel of fire in the blue mountain-girdle of Feou-liang.

Before his time indeed the Spirit of the Furnace had being; had issued from the Infinite Vitality; had become manifest as an emanation of the Supreme Tao. For Hoang-ti, nearly five thousand years ago, taught men to make good vessels of baked clay; and in his time all potters had learned to know the god of Oven-fires, and turned their wheels to the murmuring of prayer. But Hoang-ti had been gathered unto his fathers for thrice ten hundred years before that man was born destined by the Master of Heaven to become the Porcelain-God.

And his divine ghost, ever hovering above the smoking and the toiling of the potteries, still gives power to the thought of the shaper, grace to the genius of the designer, luminosity to the touch of the enamellist. For by his heaven-taught wisdom was the art of porcelain created; by his inspiration were accomplished all the miracles of Thao-yu, maker of the *Kia-yu-ki*, and all the marvels made by those who followed after him –

All the azure porcelains called *You-kouo-thien-tsing*: brilliant as a mirror, thin as paper of rice, sonorous as the melodious stone *Khing*, and coloured, in obedience to the mandate of the Emperor Chi-tsong, 'blue as the sky is after rain, when viewed through the rifts of the clouds'. These were, indeed, the first of all porcelains, likewise called *Tchai-yao*, which no man, howsoever wicked, could find courage to break, for they charmed the eye like jewels of price –

And the *Jou-yao*, second in rank among all porcelains, sometimes mocking the aspect and the sonority of bronze, sometimes blue as summer waters, and deluding the sight with mucid appearance of thickly floating spawn of fish –

And the *Kouan-yao*, which are the Porcelains of Magistrates, and third in rank of merit among all wondrous porcelains, coloured with colours of the morning – skyey blueness, with the rose of a great dawn blushing and bursting through it, and long-limbed marsh-birds flying against the glow;

Also the *Ko-yao* – fourth in rank among perfect porcelains – of fair, faint, changing colours, like the body of a living fish, or made in the likeness of opal substance, milk mixed with fire; the work of Sing-I, elder of the immortal brothers Tchang;

Also the *Ting-yao* – fifth in rank among all perfect porcelains – white as the mourning garments of a spouse bereaved, and beautiful with a trickling as of tears – the porcelains sung of by the poet Son-tong-po;

Also the porcelains called *Pi-se-yao*, whose colours are called 'hidden', being alternately invisible and visible, like the tints of ice beneath the sun – the porcelains celebrated by the far-famed singer Sin-in;

Also the wondrous *Chu-yao* – the pallid porcelains that utter a mournful cry when smitten – the porcelains chanted of by the mighty chanter, Thou-chao-ling;

Also the porcelains called *Thsin-yao*, white or blue, surface-wrinkled as the face of water by the fluttering of many fins . . . And ye can see the fish!

Also the vases called *Tsi-hong-khi*, red as sunset after a rain; and the *T'o-t'ai-khi*, fragile as the wings of the silkworm-moth, lighter than the shell of an egg;

Also the *Kia-tsing* – fair cups pearl-white when empty, yet, by some incomprehensible witchcraft of construction, seeming to swarm with purple fish the moment they are filled with water;

Also the porcelains called *Yao-pien*, whose tints are transmuted by the alchemy of fire; for they enter blood-crimson into the heat, and change there to lizard-green, and at last come forth azure as the cheek of the sky;

Also the *Ki-tcheou-yao*, which are all violet as a summer's night; and the *Hing-yao* that sparkle with the sparklings of mingled silver and snow;

Also the *Sieouen-yao* – some ruddy as iron in the furnace, some diaphanous and ruby-red, some granulated and yellow as the rind of an orange, some softly flushed as the skin of a peach;

Also the *Tsoui-khi-yao*, crackled and green as ancient ice is; and the *Tchou-fou-yao*, which are the Porcelains of Emperors, with dragons wriggling and snarling in gold; and those *yao* that are pink-ribbed and have their angles serrated as the claws of crabs are;

Also the *Ou-ni-yao*, black as the pupil of the eye, and as lustrous; and the *Hou-tien-yao*, darkly yellow as the faces of men of India; and the *Ou-kong-yao*, whose colour is the dead-gold of autumn leaves;

Also the *Long-kang-yao*, green as the seedling of a pea, but bearing also paintings of sun-silvered cloud, and of the Dragons of Heaven;

Also the *Tching-hoa-yao* – pictured with the amber bloom of grapes and the verdure of vine-leaves and the blossoming of poppies, or decorated in relief with figures of fighting crickets;

Also the *Khang-hi-nien-ts'ang-yao*, celestial azure sown with star-dust of gold; and the *Khien-long-nien-thang-yao*, splendid in sable and silver as a fervid night that is flashed with lightnings.

Not indeed the *Long-Ouang-yao* – painted with the lascivious *Pi-hi*, with the obscene *Nan-niu-sse-sie*, with the shameful *Tchun-hoa*, or 'Pictures of Spring'; abominations created by command of the wicked Emperor Moutsong, though the Spirit of the Furnace hid his face and fled away;

But all other vases of startling form and substance, magically articulated, and ornamented with figures in relief, in cameo, in transparency – the vases with orifices belled like the cups of flowers, or cleft like the bills of birds, or fanged like the jaws of serpents, or pink-lipped as the mouth of a girl; the vases flesh-coloured and purple-veined and dimpled, with ears and with earrings; the vases in likeness of mushrooms, of lotos-flowers, of lizards, of horse-footed dragons woman-faced; the vases strangely translucid, that simulate the white glimmering of grains of prepared rice, that counterfeit the vapoury lace-work of frost, that imitate the efflor-escences of coral –

Also the statues in porcelain of divinities: the Genius of the Hearth; the Long-pinn who are the Twelve Deities of Ink; the blessed Lao-tsu, born with silver hair; Kong-fu-tse, grasping the scroll of written wisdom; Kouan-in, sweetest Goddess of Mercy, standing snowy-footed upon the heart of her golden lily; Chi-nong, the god who taught men how to cook; Fo, with long eyes closed in meditation, and lips smiling the mysterious smile of Supreme Beatitude; Cheou-lao, god of Longevity, bestriding his aerial steed, the white-winged stork; Pou-t'ai, Lord of Contentment and of Wealth, obese and dreamy; and that fairest Goddess of Talent, from whose beneficent hands eternally streams the iridescent rain of pearls.

*   *   *

And though many a secret of that matchless art that Pu bequeathed unto men may indeed have been forgotten and lost forever, the story of the Porcelain-God is remembered; and I doubt not that any of the aged *Jeou-yen-liao-kong*, any one of the old blind men of the great potteries, who sit all day grinding colours in the sun, could tell you Pu was once a humble Chinese workman, who grew to be a great artist by dint of tireless study and patience and by the inspiration of Heaven. So famed he became that some deemed him an alchemist, who possessed the secret called *White-and-Yellow*, by which stones might be turned into gold; and others thought him a magician, having the ghastly power of murdering men with horror of nightmare, by hiding charmed effigies of them under the tiles of their own roofs; and others, again, averred that he was an astrologer who had discovered the mystery of those Five Hing which influence all things – those Powers that move even in the currents of the star-drift, in the milky *Tien-ho*, or River of the Sky. Thus, at least, the ignorant spoke of him; but even those who stood about the Son of Heaven, those whose hearts had been strengthened by the acquisition of wisdom, wildly praised the marvels of his handicraft, and asked each other if there might be any imaginable form of beauty which Pu could not evoke from that beauteous substance so docile to the touch of his cunning hand.

And one day it came to pass that Pu sent a priceless gift to the Celestial and August: a vase imitating the substance of ore-rock, all aflame with pyritic scintillation – a shape of glittering splendour with chameleons sprawling over it; chameleons of porcelain that shifted colour as often as the beholder changed his position. And the Emperor, wondering exceedingly at the splendour of the work, questioned the princes and the mandarins concerning him that made it. And the princes and the mandarins answered that he was a workman named Pu, and that he was without equal among potters, knowing secrets that seemed to have been inspired either by gods or by demons. Whereupon the Son of Heaven sent his officers to Pu with a noble gift, and summoned him unto his presence.

So the humble artisan entered before the Emperor, and having performed the supreme prostration – thrice kneeling, and thrice nine times touching the ground with his forehead – awaited the command of the August.

And the Emperor spake to him, saying: 'Son, thy gracious gift hath found high favour in our sight; and for the charm of that offering we have bestowed upon thee a reward of five thousand silver *liang*. But thrice that sum shall be awarded thee so soon as thou shalt have fulfilled our behest. Hearken, therefore, O matchless artificer! It is now our will that thou make for us a vase having the tint and the aspect of living flesh, but – mark well our desire! – *of flesh made to creep by the utterance of such words as poets utter – flesh moved by an Idea, flesh horripilated by a Thought!* Obey, and answer not! We have spoken.'

*   *   *

Now Pu was the most cunning of all the *P'ei-se-kong* – the men who marry colours together; of all the *Hoa-yang-kong*, who draw the shapes of vase-decoration; of all the *Hoei-sse-kong*, who paint in enamel; of all the *T'ien-thsai-kong*, who brighten colour; of all the *Chao-lou-kong*, who watch the furnace-fires and the porcelain-ovens. But he went away sorrowing from the Palace of the Son of Heaven, notwithstanding the gift of five thousand silver *liang* which had been given to him. For he thought to himself: 'Surely the mystery of the comeliness of flesh, and the mystery of that by which it is moved, are the secrets of the Supreme Tao. How shall man lend the aspect of sentient life to dead clay? Who save the Infinite can give soul?'

Now Pu had discovered those witchcrafts of colour, those surprises of grace, that make the art of the ceramist. He had found the secret of the *feng-hong*, the wizard flush of the Rose; of the *hoa-hong*, the delicious incarnadine; of the mountain-green called *chan-lou*; of the pale soft yellow termed *hiao-hoang-yeou*; and of the *hoang-kin*, which is the blazing beauty of gold. He had found those eel-tints, those serpent-greens, those pansy-violets, those furnace-crimsons, those carminates and lilacs, subtle as spirit-flame, which our enamellists of the Occident long sought without success to reproduce. But he trembled at the task assigned him, as he returned to the toil of his studio, saying: 'How shall any miserable man render in clay the quivering of flesh to an Idea – the inexplicable horripilation of a Thought? Shall a man venture to mock the magic of that Eternal Moulder by whose infinite power a million suns are shapen more readily than one small jar might be rounded upon my wheel?'

*   *   *

Yet the command of the Celestial and August might never be disobeyed; and the patient workman strove with all his power to fulfil the Son of Heaven's desire. But vainly for days, for weeks, for months, for season after season, did he strive; vainly also he prayed unto the gods to aid him; vainly he besought the Spirit of the Furnace, crying: 'O thou Spirit of Fire, hear me, heed me, help me! How shall I – a miserable man, unable to breathe into clay a living soul – how shall I render in this inanimate substance the aspect of flesh made to creep by the utterance of a Word, sentient to the horripilation of a Thought?'

For the Spirit of the Furnace made strange answer to him with whispering of fire: '*Vast thy faith, weird thy prayer! Has Thought feet, that man may perceive the trace of its passing? Canst thou measure me the blast of the Wind?*'

*   *   *

Nevertheless, with purpose unmoved, nine-and-forty times did Pu seek to fulfil the Emperor's command; nine-and-forty times he strove to obey the behest of the Son of Heaven. Vainly, alas! did he consume his substance; vainly did he expend his strength; vainly did he exhaust his knowledge: success smiled not upon him; and Evil visited his home, and Poverty sat in his dwelling, and Misery shivered at his hearth.

Sometimes, when the hour of trial came, it was found that the colours had become strangely transmuted in the firing, or had faded into ashen pallor, or had darkened into the fuliginous hue of forest-mould. And Pu, beholding these misfortunes, made wail to the Spirit of the Furnace, praying: 'O thou Spirit of Fire, how shall I render the likeness of lustrous flesh, the warm glow of living colour, unless thou aid me?'

And the Spirit of the Furnace mysteriously answered him with murmuring of fire: '*Canst thou learn the art of that Infinite Enameller who hath made beautiful the Arch of Heaven – whose brush is Light; whose paints are the Colours of the Evening?*'

Sometimes, again, even when the tints had not changed, after the pricked and laboured surface had seemed about to quicken in the heat, to assume the vibratility of living skin – even at the last hour all the labour of the workers proved to have been wasted; for the fickle substance rebelled against their efforts, producing only crinklings grotesque as those upon the rind of a withered fruit, or granulations like those upon the skin of a dead bird from which the feathers have been rudely plucked. And Pu wept, and cried out unto the Spirit of the Furnace: 'O thou Spirit of Flame, how shall I be able to imitate the thrill of flesh touched by a Thought, unless thou wilt vouchsafe to lend me thine aid?'

And the Spirit of the Furnace mysteriously answered him with muttering of fire: '*Canst thou give ghost unto a stone? Canst thou thrill with a Thought the entrails of the granite hills?*'

Sometimes it was found that all the work indeed had not failed; for the colour seemed good, and all faultless the matter of the vase appeared to be, having neither crack nor wrinkling nor crinkling; but the pliant softness of warm skin did not meet the eye; the flesh-tinted surface offered only the harsh aspect and hard glimmer of metal. All their exquisite toil to mock the pulpiness of sentient substance had left no trace; had been brought to nought by the breath of the furnace. And Pu, in his despair, shrieked to the Spirit of the Furnace: 'O thou merciless divinity! O thou most pitiless god! – Thou whom I have worshipped with ten thousand sacrifices! – For what fault hast thou abandoned me? For what error hast thou forsaken me? How may I, most wretched of men, ever render the aspect of flesh made to creep with the utterance of a Word, sentient to the titillation of a Thought, if thou wilt not aid me?'

And the Spirit of the Furnace made answer unto him with roaring of fire: '*Canst thou divide a Soul? Nay! . . . Thy life for the life of thy work! – Thy soul for the soul of thy Vase!*'

And hearing these words Pu arose with a terrible resolve swelling at his heart, and made ready for the last and fiftieth time to fashion his work for the oven.

One hundred times did he sift the clay and the quartz, the *kao-ling* and the *tun*; one hundred times did he purify them in clearest water; one hundred times with tireless hands did he knead the creamy paste, mingling it at last with colours known only to himself. Then was the vase shapen and reshapen, and touched and re-touched by the hands of Pu, until its blandness seemed to live, until it appeared to quiver and to palpitate, as with vitality from within, as with the quiver of rounded muscle undulating beneath the integument. For the hues of life were upon it and infiltrated throughout its innermost substance, imitating the carnation of blood-bright tissue, and the reticulated purple of the veins; and over all was laid the envelope of sun-coloured *Pe-kia-ho*, the lucid and glossy enamel, half-diaphanous, even like the substance that it counterfeited – the polished skin of a woman. Never since the making of the world had any work comparable to this been wrought by the skill of man.

Then Pu bade those who aided him that they should feed the furnace well with wood of *tcha*; but he told his resolve unto none. Yet after the oven began to glow, and he saw the work of his hands blossoming and blushing in the heat, he bowed himself before the Spirit of Flame, and murmured: 'O thou Spirit and Master of Fire, I know the truth of thy words! I know that a Soul may never be divided! Therefore my life for the life of my work! – My soul for the soul of my Vase!'

And for nine days and for eight nights the furnaces were fed unceasingly with wood of *tcha*; for nine days and for eight nights men watched the wondrous vase crystallising into being, rose-lighted by the breath of the flame. Now upon the coming of the ninth night, Pu bade all his weary comrades retire to rest, for that the work was well-nigh done, and the success assured. 'If you find me not here at sunrise,' he said, 'fear not to take forth the vase; for I know that the task will have been accomplished according to the command of the August.' So they departed.

But in that same ninth night Pu entered the flame, and yielded up his ghost in the embrace of the Spirit of the Furnace, giving his life for the life of his work – his soul for the soul of his Vase.

And when the workmen came upon the tenth morning to take forth the porcelain marvel, even the bones of Pu had ceased to be; but lo! the Vase lived as they looked upon it: seeming to be flesh moved by the utterance of a Word, creeping to the titillation of a Thought. And whenever tapped by the finger it uttered a voice and a name – the voice of its maker, the name of its creator: PU.

*   *   *

And the son of Heaven, hearing of these things, and viewing the miracle of the vase, said unto those about him: 'Verily, the Impossible hath been wrought by the strength of faith, by the force of obedience! Yet never was it our desire that so cruel a sacrifice should have been; we sought only to know whether the skill of the matchless artificer came from the Divinities or from the Demons – from heaven or from hell. Now, indeed, we discern that Pu hath taken his place among the gods.' And the Emperor mourned exceedingly for his faithful servant. But he ordained that godlike honours should be paid unto the spirit of the marvellous artist, and that his memory should be revered forevermore, and that fair statues of him should be set up in all the cities of the Celestial Empire, and above all the toiling of the potteries, that the multitude of workers might unceasingly call upon his name and invoke his benediction upon their labours.